GUNS OF THE ALAMO

Center Point
Large Print

Also by Bradford Scott and available from
Center Point Large Print:

Gunsmoke on the Rio Grande
The Hate Trail
Lone Star Rider
The Slick-Iron Trail

**This Large Print Book carries the
Seal of Approval of N.A.V.H.**

GUNS
OF THE
ALAMO

Bradford Scott

CENTER POINT LARGE PRINT
THORNDIKE, MAINE

This Center Point Large Print edition
is published in the year 2017 by arrangement with
Golden West Literary Agency.

First US edition: Pyramid Books.

This book is fiction. No resemblance is intended
between any charater herein and any person, living or
dead; any such resemblance is purely coincidental.

The text of this Large Print edition is unabridged.
In other aspects, this book may vary
from the original edition.
Printed in the United States of America
on permanent paper.
Set in 16-point Times New Roman type.

ISBN: 978-1-68324-420-2 (hardcover)
ISBN: 978-1-68324-424-0 (paperback)

Library of Congress Cataloging-in-Publication Data

Names: Scott, Bradford, 1893–1975, author.
Title: Guns of the Alamo / Bradford Scott.
Description: Center Point Large Print edition. | Thorndike, Maine :
    Center Point Large Print, 2017.
Identifiers: LCCN 2017010243| ISBN 9781683244202 (hardcover : alk.
paper) | ISBN 9781683244240 (pbk. : alk. paper)
Subjects: LCSH: Large type books. | GSAFD: Western stories.
Classification: LCC PS3537.C9265 G855 2017 | DDC 813/.54—dc23
LC record available at https://lccn.loc.gov/2017010243

ONE

The Indians of Texas, who learned much from the Spaniards besides the doctrines piously expounded by the padres, had a word for it which translated into "drunken-old-man-going-home-at-night." It fitted.

Later-coming gentlemen of Anglo-American descent and odd senses of humor had a couple of words characterizing the town through which the aforementioned river meandered. They called it "Unsainted Anthony."

Which would have probably shocked the good padre, Father Massanet, who set up a cross on the riverbank, erected an arbor of cottonwood boughs under which to say mass and christened his embryo settlement San Antonio.

And just as the Indians' appellation described the San Antonio River with singular aptness, so did the ribald misnomer portray the city of San Antonio. The river, spanned by some forty bridges and never in a hurry, travels fifteen miles to cross six miles of city blocks. And a great many of the gentlemen who lived in, or made San Antonio their headquarters or stopping-off point, were certainly not sainted.

Ranger Walt Slade, he whom the Mexican *peons* of the Rio Grande river villages named

5

El Halcon—The Hawk—chuckled as he gazed at the star-dimpled waters, being familiar with both legends.

But that placid water held some grim secrets and kept them well. More than a few bodies had been fished out of it. How they got there nobody seemed to know and there was a tendency not to ask too many questions about them; such curiosity sometimes proved unhealthy.

Slade turned from the river and strolled along Travis Street. He had reached a crossing when from around the corner came a woman's scream, high-pitched, horror-filled, followed by shriek on shriek of agony and terror. Slade bounded to the corner and whipped around it, unsheathing one of his long-barrelled Colts as he did so.

A few yards distant a girl was struggling madly in the arms of a man. Two more men held a fourth helpless, while a fifth man plunged a knife into his body, stroke on stroke. Blood gushed from the wounds.

The man with the knife whirled at the sound of Slade's step and lunged at him; but before the blood-smeared blade could reach its intended victim, the heavy barrel of the Colt crashed against his skull and stretched him senseless on the ground. His companions went for the guns at their belts. The street rocked to the roar of sixshooters.

Seconds later, Walt Slade, blood trickling down his face, three bullet holes in the left sleeve of his shirt, lowered his smoking guns and gazed at the five bodies sprawled on the ground.

The girl, her eyes wild, her mouth a round O of soundless terror, was crouched against a building wall.

"What's this all a—" Slade began. Before he could finish the question she darted forward and clutched his arm with frantic fingers.

"Come!" she shrilled, tugging and hauling at his sleeve. "Come! They are of the syndicate! Quick! Quick! Or you die!"

Slade hesitated, but shouts in the distance decided him; might be a good notion to be elsewhere when the shouters arrived.

Urging him to greater speed, the girl led him across the street and into a narrower and darker one. She swerved into an alley that was pitch-black, into another equally dark, and still a third.

"Faster! faster!" she panted. "They may follow."

Slade was not particularly concerned about that but he lengthened his stride to please her. She was gasping and he was breathing a trifle hard himself when they reached a broad and fairly well-lighted street. Here the girl halted and Slade for the first time took stock of his companion.

She was small and slender and nicely formed, with great dark eyes and a mass of dark hair now wildly in disarray. Not at all hard to look at, he decided.

She in turn saw a tall man, more than six feet,

with shoulders and a chest matching his height. His lean bronzed face was dominated by long, black-lashed eyes of a pale gray. His rather wide mouth, grin-quirked at the corners, modified somewhat the sternness that was almost fierceness evinced by the high-bridged nose above and the powerful chin and jaw beneath. The deep chest tapered down to a sinewy waist worked and oiled cut-out holsters, from which protruded the plain black butts of heavy guns. He wore the homely but efficient garb of the rangeland with careless grace—faded blue shirt and Levis, well-scuffed half-boots of softly tanned leather, vivid handkerchief looped at his throat. His pushed-about which were double cartridge belts supporting carefully back "J.B." revealed thick, crisp hair so black a blue shadow seemed to lie upon it.

The girl was speaking between her gasps for breath.

"You should be safe now, but you should have killed the one you struck; he will know you if he sees you again."

"Maybe I did," Slade replied. "He got quite a whack."

"I hope you did," she said, her voice vibrant. "Hurry, now, to where the lights are bright. And don't come back here."

"But what was it all about?" he asked. Without replying, she darted away into the darkness. Slade listened to the diminishing click of her high heels on the stones. Ejecting the spent shells from his guns and replacing them with fresh cartridges, he holstered the big Colts and shrugged his wide shoulders. He'd know *her* if he saw her again, and despite her warning he was coming back. A man had been murdered before his eyes. Which was of interest to the man a lot of folks opined was just a dangerous outlaw too smart to get caught and whom those who knew better declared was the ablest and most fearless of that illustrious body of peace officers, the Texas Rangers.

He swabbed his bullet-grazed cheek with a handkerchief, decided the bleeding had about stopped, shook his head over the damage done to his shirtsleeve and headed for the business section of the town.

At the intersection of West Commerce and Soledad Streets, Slade paused. Here was the notorious "Fatal Corner," where had occurred six major homicides. On this site stood the Jack Harris Vaudeville Theatre, in which took place the killing of Ben Thompson and King Fisher, both widely known outlaws and gunmen of repute, and the fatal wounding of Jack Foster, one of the theatre's proprietors. Nearby was an ornate saloon. Slade thought a drink was in order, and something to eat. He entered and made his way to the bar. This, the Calaorra, Slade knew, was one of San Antonio's most popular drinking establishments. Behind the carved and polished bar, as in many of the town's

9

similar emporiums, flashily dressed bartenders mixed fiery drinks and dodged when bullets flew. At the gaming tables men whose herds ranged over millions of acres played recklessly for high stakes against cold-eyed professional gamblers and each other. Here were combined the ingredients, wine, women and song. But the wine was hard liquor, the women were questionable, and the song was too frequently interrupted by the deadly explosion of a sixgun. San Antonio held liberal ideas as to what constituted amusement, and catered to a broad variety of tastes. Unsainted Anthony was not so much of a misnomer as it might have been.

Sipping his drink, Slade studied the big room. It was lively and gay and, at the moment, quite peaceful. But he decided there was plenty of dynamite lying loose that could easily be touched off. He found the place decidedly to his liking.

The bartender who served him was loitering nearby, waiting for him to ask for a refill. Slade suddenly shot a question at him.

"What's the syndicate?"

The barkeep's eyes widened, his mouth opened slightly and he wet his lips nervously with the tip of his tongue.

"Don't know what you're talking about," he muttered, and hurried away.

Slade studied his back retreating down the bar, a thoughtful expression in his gray eyes.

"But he *does* know," he told himself. "And my

question scared the daylights out of him. Now what have I stumbled onto?"

A second barkeep sauntered up and Slade thought his gaze was dubious. He refilled his glass without comment. Slade did not repeat his question. He finished his drink and walked to a vacant table, where he ordered a meal. Nearby was a poker table and the tenseness of the players hinted at high stakes. There was a house dealer and six players at the table. Four of them, Slade judged from their dress, were ranch owners. The other two were obviously professional gamblers, wooden-faced, quiet, wearing the funeral black relieved only by the snow of their ruffled shirt fronts, the garb usually to the liking of their fraternity. Not shifty tinhorns but men who made gaming their profession and could most often be depended on to play squarely.

One of the cattlemen interested Slade. He was a big man with wide, thick shoulders, a barrel chest, abnormally long arms and huge hands covered with black hair. The hair of his head was grizzled, his eyes under a broad white forehead were black and snapping, his mouth tight but well shaped. Slade estimated his age at about forty, perhaps a little more. He was the sort of individual who stood out in a crowd. He had the look of a hard man and very likely was.

Slade's order arrived and he turned his attention from the poker game to his food. He ate in leisurely fashion, surveying his surroundings the while, a habit with El Halcon. His attention was caught by a tall, slender, gray-haired man who was making his way around the room, pausing whenever he approached one of the waiters and apparently asking a question, and each time receiving a negative shake of the head in reply. Slade was struck by the rhythmic perfection of his movement; he seemed to glide rather than walk. He had regular features and keen, pale eyes. Altogether he gave the appearance of a successful and masterful man. Slade deduced rightly that he was the owner of the establishment. At the moment he looked decidedly irritated about something.

The gray-haired man drew near the poker table and paused. The big cattleman glanced up and caught his eye.

"What's the matter, Norm?" he asked in rumbling tones. "You 'pear sorta upset."

"I am upset, Mr. Dawson," the other replied, his voice pleasantly respectful. "Carter, my head bartender, hasn't showed up, and this is the busiest night of the week. Nobody else can mix a drink to please some of my best customers, who'll be here after the theatre, like Carter does. I can't imagine what's holding him up."

"Maybe he made a mistake and took a snort or two of the rattler juice you sell for whiskey," Dawson suggested jovially. "No wonder he hasn't showed up."

The saloon owner smiled. "I rather doubt it," he said. "I'm afraid something might have happened to him; he's not the sort to let me down on a busy night."

"Oh, he'll amble in soon, the chances are," Dawson said, peeping at his hole card. He gestured to one of his companions. "Tom," he said, "I want you to know Norman Allen, who owns this shebang. Norm, this is Tom Bledsoe, a friend of mine who has a spread over Beaumont way. Tom hasn't been here before."

"Glad to know any friend of Mr. Dawson's," Allen said heartily. "Hope you'll be with us often, Mr. Bledsoe."

"Sort of like the place, Mr. Allen," Bledsoe replied.

"I try to run it so nice folks will like it," said Allen. "I'll send over a drink."

With a smile and a nod he turned and walked to the bar. The poker game resumed. Walt Slade rolled and lighted a cigarette and leaned back comfortably in his chair, toying with a final cup of coffee. He did not miss the swift, speculative glance the Calaorra owner shot his way as he passed the table. And he was not surprised when a little later Norman Allen sauntered his way and paused, looking him up and down appraisingly.

"Howdy," Allen said pleasantly. "First time with us?"

"Guess it is," Slade replied. He nodded to the

opposite chair. "Take a load off your feet," he invited.

"Think I will," Allen said, dropping into the chair. "I'll be on them plenty before the night's over; business is already picking up and it is early. We put on a pretty good floor show a little later. Stick around for it."

"Chances are I will," Slade replied.

Allen gestured toward the poker table. "Another gentleman over there who hasn't been here before," he announced. "I like new patrons and try to make things so they'll come back."

"The way to conduct a successful business," Slade observed.

Allen nodded. "He's from over Beaumont way, or so Mr. Dawson said," he remarked, apropos of the cattleman friend of Dawson.

"I've a notion he'll like it here, 'pears to be enjoying himself."

"Some nice people come from the Beaumont section," Allen observed.

Slade suppressed a smile, and the little devils of laughter that were usually in the depths of his eyes, cold eyes the color of a glacier lake under a stormy sky, danced. He understood perfectly that Allen was doing a little probing, endeavoring to learn something about his new patron, where he came from, and so forth. And Norman Allen, undoubtedly a man of intelligence and adroit at conversation, was due to learn that which had baffled many other folks, that Walt Slade would talk pleasantly, even volubly at times, but he wouldn't tell you anything.

Allen motioned to a waiter. "Bring us a drink," he directed, "and then put your coat on and make a round of the neighborhood bars and see if you can spot Carter. If you do, lead him in here by the ear.

"Carter's my head bartender and he's late," he explained to Slade, who nodded and did not comment.

The drinks were brought, Slade rolled another cigarette. Allen lighted a cigar. They were smoking in silence when the swinging doors opened and a stocky old man with faded but alert blue eyes and a sweeping mustache entered. On his shirt front was pinned a big nickel badge. He glanced about and walked to the table.

"Howdy, Sheriff," Allen greeted him. "Sit down and have a drink."

"Don't mind if I do," he said and sat down, shooting a questioning glance at Slade. Allen also glanced at the Ranger.

"Don't believe I caught your name," he observed. Slade supplied it.

"And this is Sheriff Crane Rader," introduced Allen. The sheriff extended a wrinkled but sinewy hand. He turned to Allen.

"Norm, when did you see Bruff Carter last?" he asked.

"Very late last night when we closed up," Allen replied. "Why?"

"Well," said the sheriff, wiping his mustache, "we picked him up a little while ago, or what was left of him, over by Travis Street, close to the river. He'd been cut to pieces."

TWO

"My God!" exclaimed Allen. "Murdered?"

"Well, I don't figure he stuck a knife into himself that many times," drawled the sheriff.

Allen stared at him and sat as a man stunned.

"By the way," continued the sheriff, "did Carter fool around with the gals much?"

"Well, I guess he was a good deal of a ladies' man all right," replied Allen.

"What gals did he play with?" asked the sheriff.

"Oh, he used to go with some of the dance floor girls," said Allen. "They all seemed to like him. I suppose there were others but I couldn't say for sure as to that. Why?"

The sheriff drew a woman's crumpled scarf from his pocket and spread it on the table.

"Found this alongside a building there," he said. "Close to where Carter's body was layin'. Ever see it before?"

Allen slowly shook his head. "Looks pretty ordinary," he replied. "Hardly the sort of thing you'd notice particularly."

The sheriff nodded. "Funny," he added ruminatively, "there was a heap of blood spattered around there. I looked over the ground with a lantern. A lot more than could have come out of Carter, cut up as he was, and covering too wide an area. He'd hardly have walked around after the knife worked on him. 'Pears he must have put up a fight and left his mark on some of the hellions who jumped him."

"You figure there was more than one?" asked Allen.

"That's my opinion," nodded Sheriff Rader. "I'd say two, maybe three gents got punctured somehow. Some folks I questioned, none of 'em close to where it happened, 'lowed they heard shooting over that way. They didn't go to see about it. Figured it might not be healthy to do so, I reckon."

"Guess they did," agreed Allen. "You can't blame them. Shooting in this town usually means trouble for anybody sticking their bill in." He shook his head sadly. "Poor old Bruff!" he said. "He was a good fellow. Sort of stubborn and 'sot in his ways,' as the saying goes; there was no backing him down when he figured himself to be right. But he was always quick to take up for anybody he thought was getting a raw deal. You think he shot one of them before they killed him?"

"If he did, I don't know what he used to do it with," the sheriff answered. "Wasn't packing a gun, so far as I could ascertain. No holster, no belt, and there wasn't any laying around. Of course he could have had one stuck under his waistband and one of the hellions he winged carried it off, but I figure that sort of unlikely. Guess the answer is he was fooling around with some other jigger's woman and the feller caught up with him."

"Yes, that could be the answer," Allen conceded, drumming the table top nervously with slender fingers. "Finding the scarf there sort of makes it look that way. Where's the body?"

"At the coroner's office," Rader replied. "Did he have any folks that you know of?"

"None that I know of," Allen answered. "I'll take care of the burial if nobody shows up."

"That's nice of you, Norm," said the sheriff. "We'll hold an inquest tomorrow. Verdict will be the same old story, 'Met his death at the hands of parties unknown. Sheriff is advised to drop a loop on the varmints.' I've been getting plenty of that sort of advice lately. Realize that makes about five killings with no apparent reason for 'em in the past coupla months? Town's getting tougher than it was in the days of King Fisher and Ben Thompson."

"Always wild and I reckon it always will be," said Allen. "Afraid you've come to a salty pueblo, Mr. Slade. Though perhaps it was just as salty where you come from."

"Lots of salty places in the world," Slade replied pleasantly. Allen's brows drew together slightly and there was an irritated look in his pale eyes. Sheriff Rader turned to Slade. His glance slid over the Ranger's torn sleeve and his bullet-burned cheek.

"Just passing through, Mr. Slade?" he asked.

19

"Haven't decided for sure," El Halcon replied. "May decide to stick around a while. 'Pears to be a nice town. Perhaps I could tie onto a chore of riding hereabouts."

Rader jerked his thumb toward the poker table. "The big feller over there is Will Dawson who owns the Triangle D spread over to the west of here," he said. "Biggest and best in the section. Owns considerable holdings here in town, too. He's usually hiring and a good man to work for. You might tackle him for a job."

"That's a notion, and thank you," Slade replied. He smiled at the old peace officer, the devils of laughter dancing in the depths of his eyes. The sheriff seemed to find the expression of the long gray eyes disquieting, for he frowned, tried to look stern, then grinned in spite of himself, a rather crusty grin, but a grin.

"I've a notion you'll get along," he said. Again his glance passed over sleeve and cheek. Slade was pretty well convinced that Sheriff Rader recognized bullet holes in cloth when he saw them. Undoubtedly he was intrigued but felt he could hardly ask questions which he very likely concluded wouldn't be answered. In which he was right.

Rader glanced at the clock over the bar. "Guess I'd better be getting back to the office," he said. "Want to come along, Norm, and take a look at what's left of Carter?"

"That's a notion," agreed Allen. "Be seeing you, Mr. Slade. Stick around for our floor show. I've a feeling you'll enjoy it."

"Chances are I will," Slade replied. He nodded to the sheriff who nodded in turn. Slade watched the pair leave the saloon together, an amused look in his eyes.

Outside, Norman Allen turned to the sheriff. "Well, what do you think of him?" he asked.

"Think of who?" countered the sheriff.

"You know who, the big fellow at the table," Allen answered.

Rader tugged his mustache. "Darned if I know what to think," he admitted. "A cold proposition, all right. Never saw such a pair of eyes. They go through you like a greased knife. We've been getting some characters here of late, but he seems about the top of the heap. What do you think?"

"Same as you, I don't know what to think," Allen said. "I tried to draw him out, as I do all unusual sorts that come into my establishment. Got exactly nowhere, just like you did."

"One thing's sure for certain," said the sheriff. "He's been in some sort of a ruckus not long ago. That cut on his cheek was made by a slug or I miss my guess, and his sleeve was shot to pieces."

"And I'll wager whoever put holes in his sleeve got some himself, not in the sleeve," Allen said grimly. "Did you notice how those two guns were slung?"

"Uh-huh, and I noticed at least one of his hands was never far from them," the sheriff replied. "Reminds me a little of a big edition of King Fisher. Wonder why he's here?"

"I've a notion we're liable to find out, and it'll be something unpleasant," Allen predicted. "Not often anybody affects me that way, but somehow that big jigger seems to spell trouble."

"You could be right," conceded the sheriff. "Civil enough spoken."

"Yes, too blasted civil," grunted Allen. "Gives you the impression that he's laughing at you and knows exactly what you're thinking. Rather, what you're going to think before you start."

Sheriff Rader chuckled. "Seems to me we're sorta paying too much mind to a chuckline-riding cowhand, which is what I reckon he is," he said. "We've got real things to think about, such as the killing of Bruff Carter. Could be just a case of woman trouble, all right, but it could be something else. Robbery wasn't the motive; Bruff's wallet, with better'n a hundred dollars in it was in his pocket, and that diamond ring he always wore was on his finger. Either the killers weren't after what he was packing or were scared off before they had time to lift it. Well, maybe we'll find out. I'd better do some finding out before long; folks are beginning to look sort of sideways at me. Killings! Robberies! Wideloopings! Wish I'd stayed following a cow's tail. This sheriffin' business ain't what it's cracked up to be."

It was Allen's turn to chuckle. "Oh, you've always done pretty well," he comforted the distraught peace officer. "I figure you'll give the hellions, whoever they are, their comeuppance, sooner or later."

"It had better be sooner," growled Rader, "or there'll be another sheriff comes election time. Here we are, let's go in and take a look at Bruff."

Slade's table was near the wall and somewhat in shadow. His meal finished and an untasted drink before him, he tilted his chair back against the wall, hooked his high heels comfortably over a rung and sat smoking and reviewing recent events. The sheriff's account of the finding of Bruff Carter's body was interesting. When Slade and the girl departed in haste, they left behind three dead men in addition to Carter, and one knocked senseless. According to what the sheriff said, when he arrived on the scene only Carter's body was in evidence. Which indicated that somebody—several somebodies—had spirited away his attackers. Slade was inclined to believe that the shouting he heard was the persons the sheriff mentioned as having heard the shooting calling to one another but prudently not approaching too near the locale of the tragedy. Meanwhile, mysterious others had stealthily appeared to bear

23

off the bodies and the unconscious man. Why? Slade considered the answer simple. Somebody didn't want Carter's killers found alongside his body. Which hinted that they would have been recognized by somebody had the sheriff packed them to the coroner's office and put them on display.

And the girl's frantic anxiety to get him away from there as quickly as possible hinted that the killers had friends stationed nearby. Which, Slade thought, rather ruled out the sheriff's assumption that Carter's killing might have been the result of a clandestine love affair with an outraged rival interrupting a tryst. The "syndicate" she mentioned? That, quite probably, was but a highfalutin' title somebody hung on an outlaw bunch operating in the section. The sheriff's remark anent quite a few recent killings indicated such a condition existing. The big question, of course, was, why was Carter killed? And in such a gruesome manner.

Lighting another cigarette, Slade pondered the quirk of chance which had caused him to enter this particular saloon of all others, where the man he saw murdered had been employed.

"Almost makes you think such things are predestined to some appointed end," he chuckled to himself. "It—for the love of Pete!"

Through a back door, the musicians who composed the Mexican orchestra were filing onto a platform behind the as yet unoccupied dance floor. After them came the dance floor girls in their low-cut, short-skirted, bespangled costumes. First of all was a small, slender girl with cloudy masses of dark hair and big dark eyes. It couldn't be! But it was. Slade had to believe the evidence of his own eyes. It was the *girl!*

THREE

Slade stared at her in disbelief. He raised a slender bronzed hand, rumpled his thick black hair, and shook his head. He lifted his glass from the table, eyed it suspiciously and took a sip. Tasted all right. Nope, the likker wasn't to blame; he was really seeing her. He emptied the glass, motioned to a nearby waiter for a refill; he felt that he needed it. This was playing coincidence a mite too far.

However, a moment's reflection provided a fairly logical explanation. Carter had worked here, so it was not so farfetched that the girl who also worked here should have been in his company when he was killed. Slade studied her. She was a darn pretty girl, all right, far and away the best looking of the bunch, and it was not strange that Carter, who evidently had an eye for women, would have singled her out. Began to look like Sheriff Rader's surmise that Carter's killing was the result of a row over a woman might have some foundation in fact.

"Well, one thing's sure for certain, little lady," he apostrophised the girl, "you're not going to get away from me in a hurry this time. I've a notion that if you can be induced to talk, you can hand out some valuable information."

And now the glance he bent upon her was not

that of a personable young man for a nice looking girl, but the cold and calculating gaze of a Texas Ranger with a crime to solve.

The orchestra struck up a lively tune. Men started claiming the girls as partners and the dancing began. Slade waited until a couple of numbers were finished and the musicians paused for a drink. He had kept his gaze fixed on the girl and saw that she was standing near the edge of the floor not far from his table, toying with one of the spangles on her dress, her face somber and brooding. He rose to his feet and strode lithely to the dance floor and touched her on the shoulder.

"May I have this one?" he asked.

The girl turned and regarded him absently. Then her eyes widened and she gave a little gasp.

"You!" she breathed.

"Yep, it's me," Slade replied. "May I have this one?"

"You—you mustn't be seen with me," she exclaimed, her voice little above a whisper. "They'll be sure to recognize you if you are."

"I'll take a chance on 'they', whoever the devil they are," Slade answered lightly. "Shall we dance?"

"I—I can't refuse you," she replied. "That's what I'm here for."

"Let's go," Slade said, and slipped a long arm around her slender waist as the music began.

Walt Slade liked to dance, and he could dance.

And in this small girl with the cloudy hair he had found a fitting partner. She was graceful as a flower swaying in the dawn wind and it was plain that she also liked to dance.

Gradually Slade realized that they had the floor practically to themselves. The other couples had drawn back to watch their performance.

"Well!" boomed a voice that Slade recognized as belonging to big Will Dawson, the poker-playing ranch-owner, "Well, if that ain't just the finest looking pair I ever laid eyes on! Norm, sign up that young feller for your floor show."

For the first time the girl smiled, with a flash of little white teeth, and abruptly her beauty was vivid as a full-blown rose. She gazed up into his face with frank admiration. Almost instantly, however, her eyes clouded and her red lips quivered.

"It is sad to think of so fine a man being murdered," she sighed.

Slade shook with silent laughter. "It's been tried before, but nobody ever had much luck," he told her cheerfully.

She smiled again, wanly, and her eyes remained troubled.

The music stopped and was followed by applause from all over the room.

"Go it again!" shouted Dawson, who apparently had forgotten all about his poker game. Others took up the cry.

However, it was the orchestra leader who provided the real denouement. He came forward, bobbing and smiling and holding a guitar. His voice rang out, clear and penetrating.

"*Senores* and *senoritas*! If we can now but persuade *El Capitan* to *sing!*" He paused expectant, gazing at the tall Ranger.

"What's the use!" Slade muttered under his breath. "Spotted already! Next the sheriff'll come bouncing around and wanting to know what in blazes the notorious El Halcon is doing in his bailwick."

Dawson's bull bellow shook the rafters.

"Come on, feller, give us one! If Pete says so, you must be good."

Slade glanced at the poker table. Dawson was leaning forward expectantly, his eyes eager. Slade's keen mind quickly evaluated the situation. Dawson undoubtedly wanted him to sing and it might be a good idea to develop a friendship with the cattleman, who appeared to be a big man in the section. He looked down at his companion.

"Please," she said softly, her eyes glowing.

"Can't say no to a lady," Slade smiled. He took the guitar and ran his fingers over the strings with crisp power. Glancing around the suddenly hushed room, he threw back his black head and sang.

It was a simple little song. Such as lonely men sing around campfires at night or to restless cattle while slowly circling the herd. But as the great golden baritone-bass pealed and thundered under the low ceiling, cards and drinks were forgotten. The dance floor girls gazed on the tall singer as on a vision from a past the bloom of which faded in the desert of present, and envious glances were cast at his small partner who stood very close to him, her uplifted eyes fixed on his face.

The music ceased with a crash of chords and Slade stood smiling at his audience. Followed a roar of applause and shouts of "Give us another!"

Slade gave them another, short but hauntingly beautiful. Glancing toward the door he saw Sheriff Rader standing there, a quizzical expression on his lined face; but when the song ended he applauded heartily as the others.

Handing the guitar back to the orchestra leader, who bowed low and murmured thanks, Slade turned to the girl.

"Shall we dance?" he asked, and drew her close.

As they circled the floor she whispered, "Those men at the table under the window are watching us."

"Guess a good many folks are," Slade returned.

"But not the way they are," she said.

Slade, whose eyes were everywhere, had already noted the pair, heavily built, stocky men with dark faces and beady black eyes; they looked as if they might be brothers.

"Don't pay them any mind," he told the girl.

"I'm afraid," she answered.

"No need to be," Slade said. "Just keep on dancing."

When the number ended, he asked a question, "What's your name, honey?"

"Yolanda," she replied, and the way she said it reminded him of small silver bells echoing over still water.

"Yolanda," he said, letting the full force of his steady eyes rest on her face. "Yolanda, I want you to promise me something."

"I will," she instantly agreed. "What is it?"

"I'm going out for a little while," he said. "I want you to promise me not to under any circumstances leave this room till I return."

"But you are in danger," she said, her voice quivering a little.

"Don't bother your pretty head about it," he replied. "Is it a promise?"

"Yes, it's a promise," she answered.

"Okay," he said. "Be seeing you." Returning to his table he paid his score, flipped his hat from a nearby peg and sauntered to the door. The waiter, glancing at the denomination of the bill Slade handed him and comparing it to the tab, smiled and remarked to nobody in particular,

"There goes a real gent!"

As he neared the door, Slade saw from the corner of his eye that the two men by the window had risen to their feet and were leaving their table. He smiled thinly and walked out.

Strolling along Soledad, Slade watched the windows on the far side of the street. Quickly he caught the reflection of the two men trailing along after him. He passed Houston and turned into a narrower and darker street. Again he caught the reflection of the men pacing him. Directly ahead was a rather low wall which evidently shut in a garden. He lengthened his stride, turned a corner quickly and flattened himself against the wall. A moment later the two tails bulged around the corner and looked into the rock-steady muzzles of two long black guns.

"Elevate!" Slade blared at them. All the music was gone from his voice and it was like steel grinding on ice.

Two pairs of hands shot skyward. Their owners stared at him, mouths hanging open.

"Face the wall, your noses against it, your hands where they are," Slade ordered. He disarmed the pair, tossing the two guns over the wall, felt under their arms for shoulder holsters and at the backs of their necks and along their waistbands against the possibility of a knife, and found nothing. He stepped back, holstering the gun he had kept in his hand while he searched them.

"Okay," he said. "Turn around and fight."

Seeing that they were two-to-one and that

escape was impossible they fought like cornered rats. Less than three minutes later, two bloody, battered hulks were stretched on the ground abjectly begging for mercy.

"All right, I'll let you stay alive. This time," Slade told them. "Now go back to the man who sent you and tell him that when I get my hands on *him,* he'll get worse than you did. Move!"

Dabbing at his skinned knuckles with a handkerchief, he watched them lurch and stagger out of sight.

It had been no mere melodramatic gesture on his part. He reasoned that when the unsavory pair reported back to headquarters, wherever and whatever that was, a furor would be created that might well cause somebody who really counted to tip his hand, as angry and frightened men are wont to do.

From an alley across the street a man stepped into view and sauntered forward. Slade recognized Sheriff Crane Rader. The old peace officer nodded.

"Well, see that El Halcon is in our midst and acting up per usual," he said.

"Looks sort of that way, doesn't it?" Slade smiled.

"You gave those two gents a larrupin' I figure they'll remember for a while," the sheriff commented. "I was standing over there watching. Wanted to make sure there wouldn't be any outside interference."

"Thanks," Slade said. "Something like that could have happened."

"It would have been right in line with what's been happening in this blasted town of late," growled the sheriff. "The hellions seem to work in packs. By the way, how's McNelty?"

FOUR

Slade dissembled his surprise. "Fine as frog hair," he replied. "You know him?"

"For the past forty years or so," answered Rader. "Saw him a while back; he talked quite a bit about you. Said sooner or later you'd get your come-uppance if you kept on letting folks believe El Halcon is a blasted outlaw."

"He's jumped me several times about it," Slade admitted. "But working under cover as I often do, as El Halcon I can pick up information from sources a known peace officer can't tap."

"Uh-huh, fine, so long as you don't get tapped yourself by some trigger-happy sheriff or marshal, or by some gun-slinging hellion out to get a reputation for downing the famous El Halcon who's said to have the fastest gunhand in the Southwest, and who wouldn't mind plugging you in the back to get it."

"I'll take a chance," Slade replied cheerfully. The sheriff snorted.

"McNelty send you here?" he asked.

"No," Slade replied. "I was on my way back from a little chore of bridge building and busting up some skullduggery over on the Pecos River and decided to stop here for a few days. He'll know tomorrow I'm here, though, soon as I can send him a wire."

"Bridge building," repeated the sheriff. "You took engineering in college, I believe."

"That's right," Slade answered. "But shortly after I graduated, my dad died. He'd had financial difficulties and lost his ranch. I'd planned to take a postgrad after finishing college, but that became impossible at the moment and I was sort of at loose ends. I'd worked some with Captain Jim, who was Dad's friend, during summer vacations, and when he suggested I come into the Rangers for a while and study in spare time, I thought it was a good notion and decided to give it a whirl."

"Going into engineering soon?" Rader asked.

"I don't know," Slade replied. "I've already gotten more from private study during the years I've been with the Rangers than I could have from the postgrad, but Ranger work has sort of got a hold on me. I'll be an engineer eventually, I reckon, but I'll stick with the outfit for a while yet." The sheriff nodded his understanding.

"Sheriff," Slade said suddenly, "what's the syndicate?"

Rader shot him a quick glance. "You've heard about it, too, eh?" he growled. "To tell the truth, nobody seems to know exactly, or if they do they ain't talking. It's some kind of an infernal off-color outfit that's been working a sort of new wrinkle hereabouts. A couple of gents will drop in on a bar owner, saying, 'We're from the syndicate,' and demand a cut of the week's take, promising if they don't get it the feller will be in for trouble. Fellers who wouldn't pungle up have been having trouble. Bad fights start in their places with everything smashed to heck. We've picked a few of them out of the blasted snake-in-a-cactus-patch river that wanders all over town. Nothing to tie up their killing with anybody. None of the real big places have been bothered so far, except the Calaorra, Norman Allen's place. A couple braced him, and Norm and Bruff Carter pitched 'em out on their ears."

"And Carter was murdered tonight," Slade remarked thoughtfully. "Yes, it is sort of new here-abouts, in a way, but not on general principles. Curly Bill Brocius and his bunch over around Tombstone, Arizona, used to collect 'protection' money from the ranchers and miners. The same thing was tried on Colonel Goodnight up in the Panhandle. They didn't get anywhere with the Colonel, who was a cold proposition, but quite a few small owners did come across with protection money, until the Rangers went after the horned toads and smashed them. Bringing the system into town is not illogical; but if they really get a good hold they won't stop at small and isolated saloons. They'll get their hooks in other businesses as well, with a few nice little side issues like robbery and widelooping. Nothing new about their methods; institute a reign of terror and get folks afraid to talk. Then perhaps corrupt a few officials, like Brocius and the Skurlock bunch did, for instance, and they're all set to sweep in. The only way to handle that sort of a snake is to squash it before it gets big enough to make real trouble."

"Uh-huh," grunted the sheriff, "but first you got to find your snake, and I sure ain't had any luck doing that, so far. Been chasin' my tail all over the section, and getting exactly nowhere. Maybe you'll have better luck."

"Maybe," Slade conceded. "Anyhow, I figure I made a start tonight, by accident as it were."

"How's that?"

Slade told him, in detail. The sheriff swore pungently. "The snake-blooded hydrophobia skunks!" he concluded. "I hope the one you busted with your gun barrel had his skull cracked. And somebody came and packed off the bodies before I got there! Scared that somebody would recognize the sidewinders, eh?"

"And recognize who they'd been associating with," Slade amended.

"What about the gal?" Rader asked.

"I've been dancing with her, in the Calaorra," Slade replied. "She may know something, if I can get her to talk. Then again she may not— Carter may have just been seeing her home or something. Working in the same place causes that

38

to appear reasonable. But she did use the word syndicate and seemed to feel sure there were more of the bunch somewhere close, which would seem to evince some knowledge of their movements. On the other hand, it is logical to believe that the barkeeps and the dance floor girls and other saloon employees have heard plenty about the way the syndicate, as they call it, works, while not knowing anything relative to its makeup."

"That seems to make sense," agreed the sheriff.

Slade stood in thought for a moment, then,

"You should be to a certain extent familiar with conditions hereabouts," he said. "Have you any suspects?"

The sheriff hesitated before replying and appeared to be turning something over in his mind. Finally he spoke, albeit reluctantly, Slade thought.

"Yes," he said, "I have, although without anything really definite to pin it down with." He hesitated again, apparently arrived at a decision.

"Come on," he said, "let's take a little walk over to the edge of the Mexican quarter. It's west and a little south of San Pedro Creek, which crosses West Commerce Street. We'll be heading for Nueva Street where South Laredo Street crosses it. Over there is a place I'd like for you to take a look at—and the feller who runs it. Sort of a hangout for some characters that are questionable, to say the least, though I've never been able to pin any skullduggery on them. Salty jiggers all right, though they do seem to 'tend to their own business and don't monkey with other folks, so far as I've been able to ascertain. Anyhow, we'll have a look-see and you can form your own opinion. Yep, some salty ones hang out there."

"Salty jiggers are not always identified with criminal activities," Slade reminded him. "Aside from the eruptive violence common to such natures, they often draw a very sharp line when it comes to personal conduct. Some of the most honest and law abiding men I have known were wild young fellows ready for anything from a frolic to a footrace, just so it promised excitement. A nice woman packing a sack of gold on a dark night in a lonely street would be safe from them. More than safe, in fact, with them all ready to protect her from harm should occasion arise."

The sheriff nodded agreement. "I'll let you judge the bunch that hangs out in there for yourself," he repeated. "Let's go."

They crossed the bridge at W. Houston Street and continued south on Laredo. As they progressed the streets grew quieter, the lighting poorer. Sometimes lanterns hung on poles provided the only illumination, a practice long established in western mining and cow towns but which was being replaced with better facilities in such cities as San Antonio. After a while they reached West

40

Nueva Street, into which they turned. The sheriff paused before a wide window of plate glass through which seeped a soft glow. Pushing open the swinging doors they entered a large room filled with tobacco smoke and the rumble of voices that almost drowned the music provided by a very good orchestra.

"This," the sheriff said sententiously, "is *La Culebra*."

"The Snake, eh?" Slade translated with a chuckle. "Hope its fangs have been drawn."

"They haven't," the sheriff replied shortly. "Wait, and you'll see. There's room at the far end of the bar, and the feller standing at the end is Serge Kendricks, the owner."

As they neared Kendricks he turned and Slade thought he had never seen an uglier face, for the eyes were of the lightest green, the nose was broken and driven inwards, the whole countenance seared and puckered with the ill-healed scars of old wounds. Kendricks was burly and broad-shouldered and somewhat above average height. Slade thought that when his gaze rested on Sheriff Rader's face there was a hint of amusement in the strangely colored eyes. When he spoke, his voice was deep and as fierce as the growl of a beast of prey but with a singularly resonant quality. The kind of a voice that for all its rumbling did not strike unpleasantly on the ear.

"Howdy, Sheriff," he said. "Come down to throw us all in the calaboose?"

"I reckon I should, on general principles," the sheriff replied, apparently falling in with the other's humor.

Kendricks' eyes twinkled as he glanced inquiringly at Slade. The sheriff introduced them. Kendricks' huge paw enveloped the Ranger's slim hand, but as El Halcon's slender fingers coiled about his own, the saloonkeeper winced a little. It was the sheriff's turn to twinkle his eyes. However, there was an answering twinkle in Kendricks' as their hands fell apart.

"Don't often run up against a man who can out-grip me," he said frankly, rubbing his numbed fingers. "No offense meant, Mr. Slade. Just my perverted sense of humor, I suppose Rader would call it. I don't think *he* lacks a sense of humor, perverted or otherwise, although he manages to keep it pretty well covered by a gruff exterior."

"If I didn't have, this rumhole wouldn't have lasted as long as it has," the sheriff replied pointedly.

Kendricks chuckled. "Let's all have a drink," he suggested. "Excitable natures like the sheriff's are always the better for stimulants in one form or another. Name your poison, gents, I have most everything."

"All poison," grunted Rader. "I'll try that

42

combination of snake and cactus juice you call bourbon. Careful, Slade, an innocent stranger who smelt the cork of the bottle once was crippled for life."

However when the drinks were served, Slade was prompted to remark,

"I would say that Mr. Kendricks is a connoisseur of good whiskey."

To which Kendricks instantly replied, "I wouldn't claim to be aesthetically versed in any subject, even though I sell the stuff."

The sheriff looked puzzled. Slade smiled slightly and sipped his drink. There was a speculative gleam in Kendricks' eyes.

"Cowhand, Mr. Slade?" he remarked interrogatively, and casually, running his glance over El Halcon's rangeland garb.

"When I'm working at it," Slade replied, his smile broadening, for he was beginning to enjoy the verbal sparring. Kendricks grinned with a flash of crooked but very white teeth, white as Slade's own which, in contrast, were flawlessly even. He glanced suddenly to the right.

"Pardon me," he said, "the boys at that poker table in the corner are getting a mite loud." He turned and strode away purposefully, on powerful-looking, slightly bowed legs. Slade eyed his broad back thoughtfully.

"Well, what do you think of him?" asked Rader.

"I'd say a rather unusual personality," Slade

replied. "Not exactly what you'd expect to find running a Mexican quarter saloon."

"That's my opinion," grunted the sheriff. "Too darn unusual; I can't make him out."

"Not an easy chore for anybody, I venture to assert," Slade said.

"You two have got one thing in common, you both talk like a confounded dictionary," grumbled Rader. "I can't keep up with you."

Slade laughed, and studied the occupants of the big room, which was well crowded.

A majority of those present, he decided, were or had been cowhands, although he shrewdly suspected that the hands of more than one would show no recent marks of rope or branding iron. They were mostly gay, reckless young rannies, the sort that would start trouble at the drop of a hat before it hit the ground. A sprinkling, however, were older men with hard, watchful eyes. They were the sort who would finish trouble before it really got started. There were a number of Mexicans, some wearing overalls and sandals, others picturesquely garbed in black velvet upon which sparkled much silver. All wore the ubiquitous wide-brimmed sombrero, which even in the case of the humblest was encrusted with silver. Other nondescript individuals might be anything.

Altogether the kind of a potpourri that could be harmless one moment, explosively dangerous the next. Small wonder the sheriff was bothered about the place.

As to Serge Kendricks, Slade held his judgment strictly in abeyance. The saloonkeeper appeared to be an intelligent man with something of an education. That was as far as Slade was inclined to go at the moment. So far as character was concerned, Kendricks also might be anything. Slade was of the opinion that he was a hard man, but it took a hard man to successfully conduct a liquor business in such a section. And being a hard man did not necessarily mean being a lawless one.

Kendricks came back, grinning. "Turbulent young whippersnappers, but very little harm in them unless something riles them," he said, apropos of the poker players at the corner table. "Cool them down before they get started and they don't make any trouble. Let's have another drink. I'm in an expansive mood tonight, being honored by the presence of law and order as I am."

"You may not feel so darn honored some time," the sheriff predicted darkly. "Yep, I can stand another snort. That one sorta rocked me back on my heels but I've done caught my balance again. "What *do* you make that stuff of, Kendricks?"

"Made strictly under Government supervision, Department of Internal Revenue," Kendricks replied cheerfully. "Murder a few folks and set fire to a church, but don't ever try to cheat the

Government out of taxes. Do that and you're a gone goslin'. Here's how, gents."

Whether or not the fight started at the poker table, Slade was not sure. Anyhow, it was somewhere in that vicinity, and it was a lulu. To the accompaniment of shouts, curses, the smashing of furniture and the thud of blows. In a minute the whole end of the room appeared to be embroiled. Bellowing like a bull, Serge Kendricks bounded into the melee, swinging both big fists. The bartenders uttered soothing yells that were not heeded. Folks close to the door discreetly got out of there.

"I'm a law officer, am I supposed to wade into that stampede and bust it up?" wailed the sheriff.

"Leave them alone, but keep your eyes open," Slade counselled. Even as he spoke his left hand moved like the blurring flicker of a hummingbird's wing; the hanging lamps jumped to the crash of a shot.

FIVE

Half way across the room, a man who had drawn a gun doubled up with a scream of pain, gripping his blood-spurting hand between his knees. The weapon, one butt plate knocked off, lay yards distant. Slade's voice rolled in thunder through the room.

"That'll be all. I'll down the first man who makes a move. If you can't have a shindig without some sidewinder fanging, break it up. Straighten out that mess and get back to your tables and behave yourselves."

Slade had a gun in each hand now and the black muzzles, weaving from side to side, seemed to single out every man in the room for individual attention. The sheriff also had his gun out and Serge Kendricks stood over to one side with another.

The battlers, looking sheepish, began righting chairs and tables. Kendricks seized the wounded man by the collar and propelled him to the door, sending him flying with a well-placed kick.

"Go to a doctor and get patched up, you aren't killed," he roared. "And don't come back here if you know what's good for you."

Sheriff Rader turned to Slade. "See?" he said.

"Yes, I see," Slade replied thoughtfully.

"How in blazes did you come to spot that hellion pulling?" Rader asked.

"Because I expected just some such thing," Slade answered. "That fight was phony as a seven-dollar bill, staged to cover up what he had in mind."

"What did he have in mind?"

"Well," Slade said dryly, "he was lining sights with me when I let drive. Would have been a regrettable accident, of course, but that wouldn't have done me much good. I suppose I should have killed him instead of taking a chance and shooting his iron out of his hand, but there was just a faint possibility that I could have misread his intentions, although I don't think so."

Sheriff Rader swore a string of crackling oaths. "I *will* close this blasted joint sooner or later, see if I don't," he declared.

Serge Kendricks came striding back to where Slade and the sheriff stood, his eyes snapping with excitement and anger. He surveyed the Ranger with frank admiration.

"That was shooting!" he said. "Never saw anything like it. The loco lubbers! And some swab always has to teeter the gangplank. Sink 'em all! Let's have another drink." He glared around at the subdued crowd, motioned to a bartender whose hand shook as he filled the glasses.

The orchestra, which a moment before had

been conspicuous for its absence, filed out of a back room, followed by the dance floor girls, all of whom were young, some more than passably good looking. The music started and soon the row was apparently forgotten.

Sheriff Rader downed his drink and sucked the drops from his mustache.

"Getting late," he said. "Guess we'll be moseyin' along. "Much obliged for the drinks, Kendricks, and—the entertainment. I'll be seeing you."

"You're always welcome to a drink, Sheriff," said Kendricks, "but I can't promise to always have entertainment."

"I wouldn't bet on it," the sheriff rejoined dryly. "Come on, Slade."

"And good night to you, Mr. Slade," said Kendricks. "And thank you for what you did. I figure your quick action prevented what might have been serious trouble."

Again Slade sensed the mirthful gleam in his green eyes as they rested on the sheriff. Kendricks appeared to be enjoying some secret all his own that apparently had to do with the old peace officer.

Outside, Rader said to Slade, "Well, what do you think of him now?"

"I haven't made up my mind," Slade replied. "As I said, he's an unusual personality. And among possibly some other things, he has been a seafaring man some time in the course of his career."

49

"How do you figure that?" the sheriff asked in surprise.

"Because under stress and excitement he employs figures of speech peculiar to the sea," Slade explained. " 'Lubber' and 'swab,' for instance, are seldom used by landsmen. Not that it has any real significance, but it is interesting, especially so since such expressions do not appear during his ordinary conversation."

"Meaning?" asked the sheriff.

"Meaning that he may intentionally avoid their use for some reason or other."

"Could be that his seafaring past might be— unsavory, eh?"

"Not beyond the realm of possibility," Slade conceded. "However, that is nothing but conjecture based on nothing concrete. May have been away from the sea for a long time and in consequence has gotten away from colloquialisms."

"Could be," nodded the sheriff, "but I've noticed that a feller doesn't drop such things in a hurry. A cowhand usually talks cowhand talk no matter what he becomes later. By the way, do you figure anybody hereabouts has spotted you for a Ranger?"

"I hope not," Slade replied. "I've already been spotted as El Halcon, by the orchestra leader at the Calaorra. Otherwise, he would hardly have asked me to sing. Mexicans can be tight-lipped though, and perhaps he'll keep what he knows

50

to himself. Can't be sure about that. Really doesn't matter, but I would prefer my Ranger connections were kept secret. Incidentally, you did a pretty good job of covering up—even had me fooled."

"Figured you wouldn't want it noised around," the sheriff said with a chuckle. "But as I said before," he added, grave again, "as El Halcon you're fair game for hellions who wouldn't take a chance against a Ranger. Well, here we are."

Entering the Calaorra, they found the place well thinned out. The games had broken up, the orchestra was gone, the dance floor empty. A few die-hards still slouched against the bar with bored drink jugglers serving them and glancing at the clock. Norman Allen stood nearby looking indignant. And at a table sat a lonely little figure swathed in a dark cloak.

Allen looked blank for a moment when Slade entered in company with the sheriff; but his frown returned as he approached them. He gazed accusingly at the Ranger.

"Mr. Slade," he said, "I don't like for other people to give my employees orders."

"That so?" Slade replied cheerfully. "What's the matter?"

Allen jerked his thumb toward Yolanda at the table and answered in an exasperated voice,

"She refused to leave when the other girls did.

51

Said you ordered her not to until you returned. Won't budge. Why did you—"

"Norm," the sheriff interrupted, "if you'd use your head for something besides holding up your hat, you might have figured why. She was with Bruff Carter last night when he was killed."

Allen's customary aplomb forsook him completely. His eyes widened, his mouth dropped open.

"But what—how—why—" he stuttered.

"Because we believe one of the hellions got away alive and told others she was there," the sheriff broke in. "Those sidewinders could very well figure she might have recognized the killers and remembered who they associated with, that's why. Slade figured it wouldn't be exactly the sensible thing for her to go traipsin' outa here alone in the dark, and he was right. Laying a hand on a woman in this section of the world is mighty risky business and liable to make the feller who does the prime attraction at a necktie party, but desperate men will sometimes resort to desperate measures. Whoever is back of the hell raising hereabouts is apt to figure it isn't safe to have a witness to that killing running around loose. See?"

"I—I guess you're right," conceded Allen, still looking a bit dazed. "Yes, you're right. You said maybe one of poor Carter's killers may still be alive? That means there were more than one? What became of the others?"

"Pushing up the daisies, if they weren't dumped into the river, which the chances are they were," the sheriff returned noncommittally. "Guess that's enough for you to know right now. We'll all have a snort and then go to bed; it's darn near daylight."

Allen gazed at him a moment, decided any questions he might ask wouldn't be answered, and turned to the bar. Slade declined another drink and walked to where Yolanda sat and dropped into the chair opposite her.

"So you did as I told you to," he remarked. "Good girl!"

She was staring at his bruised face and torn shirt, the pupils of her eyes dilated, for he had not come off scatheless in his fist fight with the two would-be killers.

"You've—you've had trouble," she faltered. "B-because of me?"

"Not directly," Slade replied, "and it didn't amount to much. Where do you live? I'll see that you get home safely."

"In a small hotel on West Commerce Street."

"That's not too bad," Slade said. "I was afraid it was in that dark, twisty section where you left me last night. Why did you take off in such a hurry?"

The big eyes met his squarely. "Because I was

53

afraid if you were seen with me it might mean trouble for you. I don't think the man you struck got a good look at you, and the others—" she shuddered, "appeared to be dead. I was sure there were still others of them not far off, and if *they* had seen you—" her voice trailed off and the pupils of her expressive eyes seemed to dilate still more.

"By *they,* you mean the syndicate?" Slade asked softly.

She shuddered again, and lowered her voice. "Yes."

Slade glanced toward the bar. "See the sheriff has finished his drink," he observed. "Guess we'd better get out of here and give Allen a chance to close up; we can talk some more as we walk."

As they headed for the door, Norman Allen stopped them. "Sorry, Yolanda," he said. "You were right in obeying Mr. Slade. I just didn't know all the angles. See you tonight."

"I don't believe he's going to fire me after all," Yolanda said, with the ghost of a smile, as Allen turned back to the bar. "I felt pretty sure he would, a little while ago."

"I don't think you have to worry," Slade said dryly. He waved to the sheriff, who called back,

"Drop around to my office tomorrow if you get time; in the courthouse."

"I will," Slade promised.

A thought struck him. "Pardon me just a moment," he said to Yolanda. Approaching the sheriff, he drew him aside.

"Suppose you'll hold an inquest on Carter's body?"

"Tomorrow afternoon," the sheriff replied.

Slade lowered his voice. "Keep the girl out of it, and put a bug in Allen's ear," he said. "The less advertising she gets the better."

"I'll take care of it," Rader promised.

Slade glanced swiftly up and down the street as the swinging doors closed behind them, but saw nothing disturbing.

"Yolanda," he said, "just who and what is the syndicate?" He felt her slender body shiver.

"I don't know," she replied, "except that they are terrible. The whispers get around, you know, and they have all the girls and bartenders scared. I understand they approached Bruff Carter, who owned a share in the Calaorra, and demanded money. He refused to go along with them and—and as we were walking along the street last night, after watching the sunset on the river, those four men stepped from an alley. One grabbed me and held me while the others attacked Bruff. Poor Bruff! He was nice and I liked him. Oh, nothing serious, but he was good company. He was nice to all the girls and they all liked him."

"Recall ever seeing any of those four hellions before?" Slade asked.

"I think I saw two of them in the saloon night before last," she replied slowly. "I'm not sure, though. I was too frightened last night to really notice them closely."

"Something I wish to check with you," Slade said. "I didn't get much of a look at them myself and it was rather dark, but I'm of the opinion the men who killed Carter were wearing rangeland clothes."

"Yes, I'm sure they were," she answered. "Also the two I seem to recall seeing in the Calaorra. Why?"

"Because it could be important," Slade explained. "Meaning that it is not altogether a town bunch working out here. And I've a notion they'll go in for something besides extorting money from saloonkeepers and other business men."

She shot him a swift glance. "You appear rather interested in their doings, Mr. Slade," she commented.

"Well," he replied with a smile, "they tried to kill me, did they not? Which makes it not unnatural for me to take somewhat of an interest in them."

"I suppose so," she conceded. They walked in silence for a while. Abruptly she turned to face him.

"Pedro, the orchestra leader, appears to know you," she said.

"Yes?"

"Yes. Otherwise he would hardly have asked you to sing, would he?"

"I suppose not," Slade had to admit. His eyes danced a little. "Of course he might have just heard me sing somewhere."

"Well, he didn't talk as if that were all," she replied.

"How did he talk?" Slade asked.

"I hope you won't think I was forward in asking him about you, but it was not unnatural for me to be a little interested, was it, after what we went through together? I asked him if he knew you and he said he did. I asked him who you were and he said, 'He is El Halcon, the friend of the lowly. He is a strange man that many, and they are evil, do not love. That many, and they are good, do love. Where evil is, or wrong, or fear, there is El Halcon. And when he departs, evil, wrong and fear are no more. He is El Halcon. That is enough for you to know, *senorita*. It is enough for anyone to know, and be honored by knowing.'" She paused. Then, "That is all he would tell me. And," she added slowly, "I think, as does Pedro, it is enough."

"Thank you, and thank Pedro," Slade said, his cold eyes suddenly all kindness. "So you don't feel too bad about consorting with the notorious El Halcon?"

For the first time he saw laughter in her eyes

57

and realized what a pretty girl she really was.

"Quite the contrary, you should have heard what the other girls had to say," she countered.

"At every breath a reputation dies," he said smilingly.

"Not at all," she answered. "Your ears would have tingled with embarrassment had you heard. They're a good bunch. The Calaorra enjoys the reputation of being an absolutely square place. Which applies to the girls as well as the games and the whiskey. Norm Allen hires only the best and the most reliable."

"He knows how to choose 'em, all right," Slade said, with a glance of frank admiration.

She smiled, and colored prettily. "Here we are," she said.

The little lobby of the hotel was empty when they entered. Slade gave it a quick once-over and turned to his companion.

"Mind if I walk to your room with you?" he asked.

"I'd be pleased," she replied without hesitation.

When she paused at a door on the second floor, Slade noted that there was a hall bracket lamp directly opposite. "Your key," he said.

She passed it to him. Standing a little to one side, with her behind him, he fitted the key to the lock and flipped the door open. Light streaming into the small but neatly furnished and spotlessly clean room showed it untenanted.

"I don't think you really have anything to fear," he told her, "but the fact can't be denied that you tangled with a bad bunch, so I'm taking no chances with you. In you go, and sleep well; don't worry."

The big eyes looked up into his face. "You'll be at the place tonight?"

"Very likely," he replied.

"I hope so," she said.

He gazed down at her a moment. Then, encircling her slender waist with both hands he lifted her lightly to his lips. She clung to him a moment, smiled tremulously as he set her on her feet.

"Well, it's something to have been kissed," she said.

"And just what do you mean by that?" he asked.

"I think you can provide the answer," she replied. "Good night!"

Very softly, and slowly, she closed the door.

Before repairing to his room in a Dolorosa Street hotel, Slade paid a visit to Shadow, his great black horse, who had quarters in a nearby livery stable.

"Well, looks like we're in it again," he told the horse. Shadow rolled his eyes as if to say it was no choosing of his.

"Yes, we're in it," Slade repeated. "Can't stop off for a couple of days' relaxation without getting mixed up in something. We appear to have a positive genius for it."

I didn't mix into anything, Shadow seemed to say. Slade chuckled.

"Appears interesting, anyhow," he said. "And some interesting folks hereabouts. And *she's* a cute little trick," he added irrelevantly. Shadow snorted derisively and munched a mouthful of oats from his feed box. Slade tweaked his ear. Shadow bared milk-white teeth, then thrust his muzzle into Slade's hand and blew softly. Slade bestowed a final affectionate pat and left the stable. In his room he cleaned and oiled his guns, then went to bed and slept soundly til noon.

SIX

Immediately upon arising, Slade visited the railroad telegraph office, where he sent a terse and somewhat cryptic message:

Something interesting happened.

The operator gazed curiously at the address. "That all?" he asked. "No first name, just 'Mr. James'?"

"That's all," Slade replied. "Just Mr. James. You should have an answer in an hour or so; hold it for me."

After enjoying a leisurely breakfast and smoking a couple of cigarettes, Slade returned to the office, where he found Captain Jim McNelty's laconic reply awaiting him:

Keep it interesting.

Chuckling he tore the paper into little bits and cast them into a convenient spittoon.

"Guess that's it," he remarked to himself. "Here we go!"

Next Slade made his way to the sheriff's office and thence to the room where the inquest was held, Sheriff Rader accompanying him.

The inquest was short. It said that Bruff Carter met his death at the hands of parties unknown. As Sheriff Rader predicted, he was advised to get off the seat of his pants and drop a loop on the varmints.

"Darned easy to give advice, not so easy to follow it," the peace officer snorted to Slade. "Want to take a look at the body?"

Bruff Carter had evidently been a good looking man in life. Slade judged his age to be somewhere in the middle thirties. The chin had a stubborn jut to it and the mouth was firm but kindly. Very likely the kind of an individual who wouldn't stand for being shoved around. Slade gathered that he did not go to the authorities at once after rebuffing the syndicate's demand for extortion money. Which was a pity. Might have prevented the tragedy.

When they arrived at the sheriff's office they found a very angry visitor awaiting them. Will Dawson, the big poker-playing cattleman of the night before was in a roaring bad temper, and he roared.

"Two hundred head of prime beef stock rustled from my south pasture!" he stormed. "This is getting past the limit! Rader, you've got to do something about it."

"All right, I'll ride over there for a look," the sheriff replied wearily.

"What's the use of that?" snorted Dawson.

"The hellions have got hours and hours of a start. I figure it must have happened before daylight, and we didn't discover it until nearly noon. My cows are gone."

Slade, who had been an interested listener, spoke up.

"It rained real hard yesterday morning," he said. "The ground should be a mite soft and it might be possible to trail the herd and perhaps come up with it if they stop someplace for the night. Any idea which way the cows went, Mr. Dawson?"

"Where else would they go 'cept west through the hills and to the brush country to some hole-up. After that the devil knows where."

"Cows travel slowly over rough ground and through a brushy section," Slade observed. "Might be possible to catch up with them," he repeated.

"Seems to me that makes sense," said the sheriff. "What say, Will? I'll round up a posse and we'll try it a whirl."

"Never mind the posse," growled Dawson. "My boys will be rarin' to go. You can swear them in and they'll make all the posse you'll need. I told them to stick around the *casa* till I got back. You coming along, Mr. Slade?"

"If you don't mind," Slade replied.

"If you can shoot like you can sing, you may come in handy," said Dawson. He glanced at the black gun butts flaring out from the Ranger's sinewy hips.

"Got a notion you can," he added. "Let's go!"

"I'll get my horse and be with you in a jiffy," Slade said, heading for the door. He was back by the time the sheriff was ready to ride. Dawson gazed at Shadow and whistled.

"Well, that's just about the finest looking cayuse I ever laid eyes on," he said. "He's a beauty."

He stretched a hand to Shadow's nose as he spoke. Just in time Slade gripped his wrist and jerked it back. The slashing stroke of the gleaming white teeth missed by a hair's breadth. Shadow glared with rolling eyes and flattened ears. Dawson looked considerably startled.

"One-man horse, eh?" he rumbled. "I like that kind."

"It's all right, Shadow, he's a good *hombre*," Slade said. "Okay, sir, now you can pat him," he told Dawson.

"Darned if I don't believe he understood what you said," said Dawson. He reached out a tentative hand. Shadow pricked his ears and regarded him mildly and a moment later blew into the hand that stroked his nose.

"He *did* understand what you said," declared the rancher. "Well, dip me for a sheepherder!"

"Guess he did," Slade agreed. "He doesn't allow anybody to touch him unless I give the word. Now he's your friend for life."

"Unless I took a notion to take a wallop at you, then I've a notion he'd make sausage meat of me," Dawson commented dryly. "All set, Rader? Let's go."

They left town by way of West Nueva and Monterey Streets and headed west by a little south on a well-traveled trail. After an hour or so of riding over excellent cattle range dotted with fat beefs, they reached the Triangle D ranch-house, a fine big building set in a grove of cottonwoods. A score and more of cowhands were lounging around the bunkhouse and the yard.

"Saddle up, boys," Dawson told them. "We're going to drop a loop on those sidewinders. Rader will swear you in as a posse."

Another hour's riding and they reached the pasture in question. It was long and narrow. Slade gathered that Dawson's holding was shaped like the triangle for which it was named, and here was the point of the acute angle. Less than a mile distant began the wooded hills of the Edwards Plateau with the true brush country beyond. On those hills and to the west the prickly pear grew higher than the head of a mounted man, with it every type of thorny vegetation known to the Southwest; the catclaw, *huajillo*, *agarita*, *vara dulce*, *amargosa*, rattail cactus, Spanish dagger, and the shunned *junco*, which Mexicans of the region believe was woven into Christ's crown of thorns.

Here a horseman had to be able to ride almost under and alongside his horse as well as on its back, acrobatics necessitated by the dodging of clawing limbs and thorny branches.

But, Slade knew, through this inhospitable region were trails, most of them ancient, by which the terrain could be traversed even by cattle. The outlaw fraternity were familiar with those winding tracks upon which honest cowhands seldom ventured.

At a word from the Ranger, Sheriff Rader called a halt. Slade dismounted and began carefully quartering the ground. Very quickly his trained eyes detected the indubitable marks of passing cattle that had moved at a speed at variance with their usual meanderings.

"They headed west, all right," he said, forking Shadow. "Now we'll try and find where they took to the brush."

Dawson shot a significant glance at the sheriff. "Knows his business, all right," he said.

"Uh-huh, reckon he does," Rader agreed dryly. "Will, I'm getting a notion you may get your cows back."

Slade led the way to the wall of growth, alongside of which he rode slowly for a little distance, studying it intently. He paused at a spot where the brush was somewhat broken and gave the appearance of having been pushed back.

"Here we are," he said. "Let's go."

To the accompaniment of vivid profanity, the men pushed their way through the thorny tangle until they found themselves at the beginning of a depression more than a foot deep, walled on either side by the chaparral but practically free from vegetation. This strange "trench" wound up the slope ahead.

"An old Indian trail," Slade explained. "The beating of untold numbers of moccasined feet through unguessed centuries packed the earth until it shed water like stone and in consequence soured until nothing will grow on it. I've seen the like before."

"Well, I'll be hanged!" sputtered Dawson. "I never knew this darn snake track was here during all the years I've lived in the section."

"I imagine neither you nor any of your hands ever had occasion to penetrate the growth and try to ride through it," Slade observed. "Otherwise you might have hit on the trail."

"Guess that's so," agreed the rancher. "Don't see why anybody in his right mind would try to."

"Have you ever lost cows from down here before?" Slade asked.

Dawson shook his head. "Lose some up to the north every now and then, to some brush-poppin' skunks, never anything big like last night. Yep, last night was the first down this way."

"Somebody was familiar with, or familiarized himself with, the section over here," Slade commented. "I'd say he did considerable brush country riding, perhaps down to the southeast, where there's plenty of it into which the long-horns stray, and knew that these old trails exist in thorny sections. I gather that your cows are mostly improved stock which is much less liable to stray into prickly pear chaparral."

"That's right," said Dawson. "Hasn't been a longhorn hereabouts for a long time."

All the while they were riding up the winding depression at a good pace. Soon Dawson conceded that without a doubt cattle had passed that way no great time before.

"Slade, you're one smart *hombre*," he chortled. "Believe me, I ain't going to forget it."

They reached the crest of the low hill. The trail flowed across it, plunged into a wide and deep hollow and writhed up the opposite slope. Through a rift in the growth, Slade eyed the westering sun.

"I've a notion that if we have no bad luck, we may catch them up by dark or a little after," he said. "I figure they'll make camp for the night in some gulley where there's grass and water. Their logical course is to continue west for a while and then veer south toward the Nueces country, where it isn't hard to dispose of stolen cows at a good price. Believing they are not pursued, they won't push the beefs overly hard and run fat off them. Yes, we should overtake them by sundown or a little later."

"I can't wait till we do," growled Dawson. "The ornery hyderphobia skunks!"

On and on flowed the old trail. The beat of the horses' hoofs sounded loud on its hard surface. The cowboys chattered gaily among themselves, looking forward to the coming ruckus with the wideloopers as a school boy looks to a holiday. Slade, on the other hand, was quiet and watchful, carefully studying every movement of birds on the wing, the reactions of little animals they spotted in the brush from time to time. If the quarry by any chance anticipated pursuit, it would be easy to set an ambush and the pursuers might well find themselves holding the hot end of the branding iron.

Then on the crest of a hill the trail forked. The main branch continued westward, the other, narrower and much newer, veered sharply to the south.

"Now what!" barked Dawson as the posse jolted to a halt.

The westward trail was still the deep depression and hard surfaced as ever. The other fork, on the contrary, was of softer ground that had absorbed the rainfall of the day before. And on the softer soil the prints of cattle were plainly visible.

"Yep, they turned south here," said the sheriff. "Let's go!"

"Hold it!" Slade told them. He was studying the prints. "Hold it! We keep going west."

"What do you mean?" demanded Dawson. "Ain't the tracks leading south plain as the nose on your face. What do you mean we go west?"

"I mean," Slade replied quietly, "that the hellions are smarter than I gave them credit for being. They're taking no chances on possible pursuit and laid down a decoy trail to throw anybody following off the track."

"But the cow tracks!" Dawson exclaimed.

"Those tracks," Slade explained, "were made by four or five and a single rider. Anybody not paying much attention would go skalleyhooting south and end up overtaking a handful of cows browsing along, and *no* rider. Take a good look at those prints. Were they left there by two hundred cows and maybe a dozen riders?"

"I'll be hanged if he ain't right!" exclaimed the sheriff. "Uh-huh, *I* would have gone skalleyhootin' south, all right and wouldn't have caught on till it was too late. Well, if this don't take the hide off the barn door!"

"It's an old trick, but effective," Slade said. "Let's go. And from now on less talk and more listening. I'd say we're getting fairly close to them and if they hear us coming we may get a reception we won't enjoy."

At a slightly slower pace the posse rode on, alert and watchful. The sun had vanished behind the hills and the sky was ablaze with a multi-colored glory; but in the hollows the shadows were already curdling and crawling slowly up the slopes. Birds were singing their sleepy songs. The wind, as if in anticipation of the coming hour of rest, had died and not a leaf stirred. Slade knew that in the great hush, sounds would travel far and strained his ears to catch any hint that they were nearing the stolen herd.

Nearly full dark had fallen when it finally came, thin and faint with distance, the querulous bleat of a tired and disgusted steer.

"Steady!" Slade cautioned his companions. "They're not far ahead of us. Slow down to a walk till we get our bearings."

Tense and eager, the posse crept forward. Hands were poised to grab a horse's nose did it show signs of neighing. Ears were strained to catch the slightest sound.

Again came the peevish bawl, sounding much nearer.

"Stationary," Slade said. "They've stopped to bed down for the night. Keep your eyes skinned for the glow of a fire. We'll be leaving the horses before long and do the rest of the way on foot. The click of irons carries a long way on a still night."

They cautiously climbed a slope and reached the rim of a hollow, brimful of darkness.

"Hold it!" Slade exclaimed sharply. "There they are."

Below on the floor of the hollow, which was

wide but shallow, flickered a point of light that steadily grew in size.

"They're bedding down for the night," Slade said, lowering his voice. "We'll wait till they've had time to get the cows settled and are grouped around that fire preparing something to eat. Leave the horses here with a man to look after them and keep them quiet. Give the devils ten more minutes and we'll move. If it comes to a fight, and it very likely will, shoot fast and shoot straight. I figure that's a hard bunch down there and it won't do to take chances."

"We'd oughta snuck up in the dark and mow 'em down," growled Dawson.

"Peace officers must announce themselves and provide an opportunity to surrender quietly," Slade replied. "Remember, the sheriff swore us all in as special deputies."

"Guess that's so," Dawson conceded grudgingly.

"You're in charge, Sheriff," Slade reminded Rader. "You do the talking."

"Plumb forgot I was," replied the sheriff, with a creaky chuckle. "Think we can move now?"

"Let's go," Slade said, "and for Pete's sake, be quiet."

SEVEN

Silently as ghosts, but very purposeful ghosts, the posse crept down the slope. From below came a mutter of voices and an occasional harsh laugh. The tang of wood smoke spiced the air, and the tantalizing aroma of boiling coffee and frying bacon. To all appearances, the rustlers expected no interruption. Slade kept a sharp lookout for a possible guard on the trail although he hardly expected there would be one.

Now they could make out forms moving about the fire, which was built on the bank of a small stream. Farther along was the dark bulk of the feeding cattle.

"Looks like nine or ten of the hellions," breathed the sheriff. Slade nodded.

Without raising an alarm the posse reached a point just outside the ring of firelight. Slade motioned to Sheriff Rader, who took a long stride forward, El Halcon beside him. His voice rang out.

"Elevate! You're covered and under arrest!"

The astounded outlaws froze in grotesque positions, staring wide-eyed at the two figures and the shadowy forms spread out behind them. For a moment it looked like there would be no resistance.

Just in time Slade saw the firelight glint on a gun a man standing in the shadow had stealthily unleathered. He drew and shot before the rustler could pull trigger. The heavy slug, smashing through the man's breast, knocked him clean off his feet.

That was all the Triangle D cowboys needed. They had been itching to mow down the rustlers and proceeded to do so with relish and gusto. Those were stern days and there was scant mercy for malefactors caught in the very act. Judge Colt usually held court, and from "his" decisions there was no appeal.

The outlaws fought with the courage of despair. Back and forth through the gloom lanced the spurts of orange flame. The hills echoed to the uproar. The frightened cattle filled the air with their bawling. Yells, curses, shrieks of agony and the steady booming of the reports flung up to the stars in a hideous pandemonium of sound.

Ten seconds later, Slade lowered his smoking guns and strode forward ready for instant action in case some sidewinder was playing possum and waiting for a chance to fang.

But there was no movement from the twisted forms scattered about the campfire. He paused beside two bodies lying almost side by side; stocky men whose dark faces were cut and bruised and swollen. He beckoned to Sheriff Rader.

"Recognize them?" he asked. "The pair I had

74

the ruckus with over by Soledad Street last night."

"Darned if it ain't," said Rader. "You sure marked 'em up all right, but not serious enough to keep them from taking part in this skull-duggery. Guess they must have slid out of town as soon as their heads stopped buzzin'."

"Yes," Slade nodded. "Remember what I told you? That the hellions would be branching out into other fields. Your syndicate, so called, is just a regulation owlhoot bunch, but with head-quarters in town and a smart man who's ready to experiment with new angles running the outfit. Yes, a very smart man. I've a notion the community will be quite surprised when and if he's flushed from cover."

"I've a notion I won't be," growled the sheriff. "That busted-nosed hellion!"

"You have no proof that Serge Kendricks is the man we're looking for," Slade reminded him.

"Uh-huh, I've got no proof, but I've sure got suspicions," Rader retorted.

Slade himself was forced to admit that the try against his life in La Culebra the night before tended to bolster the sheriff's suspicion of Kendricks; but still there was no proof that Kendricks had anything to do with it. His judgment of Kendricks must still be held in abeyance.

"Okay," he said, "but don't go spreading them

around. If you're right, it'll just put him on his guard. If you're wrong, you'll be doing an innocent man an injustice."

"Guess you're right," Rader grudgingly conceded.

Will Dawson came striding up. "All done for, so far as I can see," he said. "Ornery looking specimens. Some of the boys 'low they're pretty sure they've seen some of 'em in town, but that's about all they can recall. No, none of our bunch bad hurt. A few punctures and some skin knocked loose. Nothing much more."

"Send for the horses," Slade directed. "I have some salve and bandages in my saddle pouches. Wait, I'll call Shadow."

He whistled a loud, melodious note. A couple of minutes later there was a drumming of hoofs on the trail and the great black appeared, snorting inquiringly. Slade patted his neck, extracted the medicants and proceeded to patch up the wounded.

"Darn critter's got more sense than the average cowpoke," Dawson chuckled with an admiring glance at Shadow.

"He wouldn't need much to have that," observed the sheriff.

"Guess that's right," agreed Dawson. "But the real terrapin-brained specimens quit following a cow's tail and get into politics and get elected to something or other."

"The way things have been going of late, I ain't arguing the point," replied Rader.

"Now what?" he asked, when Slade had finished his ministrations. The Ranger glanced around.

"Appear to be plenty of provisions spread out, and I for one could stand a small surrounding," he said.

"Me too," said Dawson. "I'm ga'nt as a gutted sparrow. Hey, you work dodgers, get a helpin' of chuck started."

The hands got busy and soon had an appetizing meal prepared, to which all did full justice.

"And now," said Slade, draining a final cup of coffee, "don't you think it would be a good idea for Mr. Dawson to assign some of his hands the chore of bringing the cows in after it gets light, while the rest of us head for town with the carcasses? We've got a long ride ahead of us but I figure we should make it by morning."

"Makes sense," said the sheriff. "Okay, boys, round up those hellions' horses and rope the bodies on 'em."

Slade had another suggestion. "Might be a good notion to go through their pockets on the chance of discovering something that might tie them up with somebody."

"The brands on the horses might tell us something, too," observed Dawson.

"Maybe," Slade admitted, "only I'll wager all

you'll find will be Mexican skillet-of-snakes burns that won't mean anything."

Which proved to be the case, and the outlaws' bodies revealed nothing of significance except a surprisingly large sum of money.

"The hellions never collected that following a cow's tail," declared Dawson. "What you going to do with it, Crane?"

"Well, I reckon it's supposed to go into the county treasury," said the sheriff. "But if you gents will excuse me, I'm going over in the bushes for a few minutes, and if somebody happens to swipe it while I'm gone, I don't reckon there's anything I can do about it."

He vanished into the darkness. Dawson, chuckling, began apportioning the money among the hands. He glanced inquiringly at Slade, but the Ranger smiled and shook his head. Dawson did not urge him to accept a share. When the sheriff returned, the spot where the coin and bills had been heaped was bare.

"Looks like we have thieves in our midst," he sighed, shaking his head regretfully. "Now if you're all finished with your stealin', gents, suppose we get going."

Progress with the led horses was slow and it was long past full daylight when the grim cavalcade wound through the streets. And then there was a to do in San Antonio. Lines of citizens filed into the coroner's office to have a look at the bodies. Several bartenders and shopkeepers were of the opinion that they had seen one or more of the outlaws in their places of business, but if they recalled anything else, they kept it to themselves.

"People are scared, especially saloon owners and their employees," Slade remarked. "They're not talking."

"Can't blame 'em, after what's been happening hereabouts of late," Rader replied.

Among those who viewed the bodies was Serge Kendricks. There was a peculiar expression in his strangely colored eyes when he spoke to Slade. However, he refrained from any comment.

"And now what?" asked the sheriff, as the crowd began to taper off.

"Now," Slade said, "I'm going to bed."

"Me, too," said the sheriff.

"I think I'll mosey over to the Calaorra and have a drink first," said Dawson. "Yes, I'm going to stay in town over night; crave a mite of relaxation. See you tonight, gents."

As Dawson was having his drink, Norman Allen approached him.

"Good morning, Mr. Dawson," he greeted. "Understand you had a successful excursion."

"Yep, plumb successful," replied Dawson. "I got my cows back, thanks to that Slade feller. He's a wonder."

Allen eyed him a moment. "Mr. Dawson," he said, "do you know who that man is?"

"Name's Slade, that's all I know or care," replied Dawson, motioning for a refill.

"Mr. Dawson," Allen said impressively, "that man is El Halcon."

Dawson stared. "The devil you say!"

"Yes, El Halcon," repeated Allen. "The notorious owlhoot and killer the law seems never able to catch up with."

"Hmmm!" said Dawson, eyeing his drink. "Might have known it when he sang the other night. The singingest man in the whole Southwest, they call him, and with the fastest gun hand. Right on both counts, I'd say."

"Yes, he has undoubtedly killed a number of people," nodded Allen.

"Guess he has," agreed Dawson. "Hope he kills some more of the same sort. More power to him!"

"Taking the law into one's own hands is questionable, to say the least," observed Allen.

"Not when the law falls down on the job," retorted Dawson.

"Anyhow I thought I should tell you," said Allen. "Seeing as he is hardly the kind of person a reputable cattleman would care to associate with."

"That so?" replied Dawson, with dangerous quiet. Allen apparently did not note the sparkle in his snapping black eyes, for he continued.

80

"Yes, there's no doubt but he's El Halcon."

"What if he is!" roared Dawson, with a sudden blast of anger. "Who gives a blankety-blank-blank! For me he's the bully boy with a glass eye, and anybody who says something against him has me to contend with, and don't you forget it."

"I meant no offense," Allen answered. "I was merely voicing a friendly warning."

"Keep your warnings to yourself," growled Dawson, tossing off his drink. "I'll take a chance on him. So long, I'm going to bed."

There was a speculative gleam in Allen's pale eyes as he watched the swinging doors close on the rancher's broad back.

"You may be taking a good deal more of a chance than you think, Mr. Dawson," he said aloud but very softly.

EIGHT

It was near sunset when Slade awoke feeling greatly refreshed. For some minutes he lay sleepily conning over recent events. Altogether they were fairly satisfactory. Looked like the syndicate was being thinned out a bit, at least. That is if the wideloopers were members of that mysterious organization, and he believed they were. However, he was not so sanguine as to think the syndicate had suffered any appreciable damage. Such a snake grows a new body mighty fast, so long as the head is active, and at the present he hadn't the slightest notion who the head could be. Serge Kendricks might be classified as an obvious suspect, but Slade had long since learned to distrust the obvious.

Just the same, the head must have suffered something of a jolt during the past few days. There were nine bodies reposing peacefully in the coroner's office. The three cashed in the night of Bruff Carter's murder made an even dozen. Which was rather more than even a big outfit could view with equanimity.

Slade knew, though, that he'd have to watch his step or he might well make it a baker's dozen, and he had no desire to be "unlucky thirteen" on the list of San Antonio's recently departed.

There was little doubt but that he had already been or would be recognized as El Halcon with a reputation for horning in on good things other folks had started and skimming off the cream. The syndicate would be a bit put out, mildly speaking, by his presence in the section and the attendant happenings. The word would have gone out to get the horned toad and get him fast.

But the very probable organized effort to do away with him did not bother him much. If his number wasn't up, nobody could put it up, and the very fact that the syndicate would consider him only a smart owlhoot bent on encroaching on their preserves would quite likely cause them to take chances they wouldn't take against a known peace officer. It had happened that way before. So he arose in a cheerful frame of mind.

After bathing and shaving, he decided that some breakfast was in order and set out to fill that innermost need. He was about to turn his steps toward the Calaorra when he abruptly changed his mind. He'd eat at La Culebra and thus have an opportunity to give the place a leisurely once-over.

It was a pleasant evening and Slade enjoyed the walk to West Nueva Street. On the bridge across San Pedro Creek he paused for a moment and gazed down at the placid water, then continued on his way.

It was still early when he reached La Culebra

and there weren't many patrons present. Some Mexicans were playing monte in a desultory fashion. A few young cowhands lounged at the bar. At a corner table two elderly gentlemen who had the look of prosperous businessmen were enjoying a meal.

He was evidently remembered from his previous visit, for the bartenders waved at him and the waiter who came to take his order nodded and smiled.

La Culebra was not so ornate as the Calaorra and more in line with Border country saloons. There was a long bar, a lunch counter with tables for customers who preferred to take their food in a more leisurely manner, a number of card tables, a faro bank and two roulette wheels. The dance floor was commodious, with a raised platform in the rear for the accommodation of the orchestra. Everything was spotlessly clean.

Serge Kendricks was not in evidence, but as Slade waited for his food to be prepared, he entered. Making his way to the end of the bar he conferred with a bartender for a few minutes, glanced at some papers tendered him and then gazed about the room. Spotting Slade, he made his way to the table.

"Mind if I join you?" he asked. "I haven't had any breakfast, either."

"Will be a pleasure," Slade replied.

Kendricks dropped into a chair and gave his

84

order to the waiter. He regarded Slade, a twinkle in the depths of his green eyes. Slade abruptly realized that Kendricks' ugliness of feature was the type of ugliness that makes no lasting impression on the viewer and was not at all repulsive.

"Well, Mr. Sladc, it would seem you've raised hell and shoved a chunk under a corner since you dropped anchor in this port," he remarked.

"Somewhat of an exaggeration, I'd say," Slade replied smilingly. "And for a while it looked like I might end up laid on my beam-ends."

Kendricks chuckled and the twinkle became more pronounced. "Don't miss much, do you?" he said. "Yes, I was on the sea for a few years. Try to forget the talk, which is hardly fitting to cow country, but it slips out now and then. I was first mate on a pearling schooner for a while. Off the Carolines the Lascar crew mutinied. Was quite a shindig while it lasted. I got belted across the nose with a belaying pin and slashed a few times, with a wavy edged kris. Left me real pretty."

"I don't think you need to let it worry you," Slade replied, and meant it.

"Oh, it doesn't," Kendricks said cheerfully. "Gives me a nice tough look, which is an asset in this business. You appear to have stayed pretty well unscarred for one who lives an adventuresome life."

"What makes you think I do?" Slade parried. Kendricks grinned.

"El Halcon has that sort of a reputation, I believe," he countered. "Oh, I'm not psychic or a mind reader; it's all over town. Sure has got a lot of folks buzzing. Doesn't appear to affect Sheriff Rader much; I'm of the opinion he isn't much given to judging from hearsay, even if he does look sort of sideways at me."

"I gather your place here is—rather turbulent at times, which would tend to prejudice a peace officer," Slade observed evasively.

Kendricks chuckled again, and didn't deny it. Immediately, however, he was grave.

"Mr. Slade," he said, "I spoke rather facetiously about you being known as El Halcon, but I wish to warn you, although I guess you know it already, that you have made some dangerous enemies here who will spare no pains to— eliminate you, if possible."

"I'll try not to be—eliminated," Slade smiled. Kendricks grinned.

"I've a notion we have kindred philosophies," he said. "What is to be will be and there's no stopping it."

"Yes," Slade said. "But I also maintain that we can, to a certain extent, at least, direct events by personal initiative, and that we are not freed of personal responsibility. We use the expression, 'if our number isn't up, nobody can put it up,' but we ourselves can put it up by our own personal actions. We can rise to the heights or sink to

86

the depths dormant in our own nature. That I implicitly believe."

"I'm inclined to agree with you," Hendricks said. "You portray the subject graphically and with clarity. It's a pleasure to converse with you, Mr. Slade. I seldom contact anyone capable of discussing such matters intelligently. Rather out of the ordinary for a—cowhand."

"Or a—saloonkeeper," Slade smiled.

Kendricks' eyes twinkled. "Here comes the chuck," he said, "let's eat."

While they were eating, the orchestra filed onto the platform. The dance floor girls followed. Which turned Slade's thoughts to Yolanda. He hoped she was all right, and felt pretty sure she was. He'd see her later in the evening.

Slade left La Culebra in a more uncertain frame of mind than when he had entered. Serge Kendricks was a good deal of an enigma, and conversation had done little to dispel the aura of mystery that surrounded him.

One angle Slade considered of significance. The methods employed by the syndicate were somewhat novel to this section of the country, hinting that they were imported from elsewhere. And there was scant doubt but that Serge Kendricks had been around. Aside from mentioning that he had been on the sea, he had divulged no information relative to himself, and had deftly parried Slade's veiled suggestion that he do so.El Halcon was not often baffled in a contest of wits, but Kendricks was singularly adept at repartee and the Ranger felt that he had gotten exactly nowhere in the course of their bout.

Of course the explanation could be simple. Kendricks might well be a bit chary of going too deeply into personal matters with a man of El Halcon's reputation. He knew that his reasons for being in San Antonio were open to question by a good many people. Including, he hoped, the members of the syndicate. Not knowing just what he was dealing with, it was not strange that Kendricks should be somewhat on his guard.

Well, if Kendricks was equally puzzled about *him,* curiosity or, had he anything to conceal, apprehension might cause him to make a slip. Slade dismissed the problem for the moment and headed for the Calaorra.

He found Will Dawson ensconced at a poker table. Sheriff Rader was not in evidence. Norman Allen smiled and nodded but did not approach him. Slade found a place at the bar and ordered a drink. Curious glances were cast in his direction and with amusement he noted a drawing together of heads.

An individual with the appearance of a prosperous businessman strolled up from the end of the bar and looked Slade up and down with shrewd eyes.

"Howdy, son. I'm Phil Watkins," he announced. "I own the Emporium General Store on Commerce Street."

"How are you, Mr. Watkins?" Slade replied as they shook hands.

"Feeling pretty good today, better'n I have for a spell," the other replied. He looked Slade over again. "Son," he said, "I've been hearing things about you, but after the way you downed three of those varmints who killed poor Bruff Carter and lent Bill Dawson a hand yesterday, I'm here to tell you I'm for you till the last brand is run. And that goes for a lot of other folks. You've done more against those hellions in a few days than anybody else has managed to do since they started oper-ating. Fact is, some of us fellers plan to go to Crane Rader and suggest that he make you a deputy with the special chore of running down the hellions. This thing has got to be nipped in the bud. So far, they've only tackled saloonkeepers and such, but once they begin to really feel their oats, nobody will be safe. Yes, we're going to Rader, and I feel sure the Commissioners will string along with us. What do you say, son, are you available?"

"Official backing is not to be discounted," Slade replied, smiling slightly.

"Fine!" exclaimed Watkins. "We'll get it all

fixed up in a few days." He chortled delightedly. "El Halcon a deputy sheriff! Wonder what those sidewinders will think?"

Slade could predict with great confidence what the sidewinders would think. They'd think it was a smart move on the part of the blasted owlhoot who had wormed his way into the sheriff's confidence and would henceforth have official sanction for whatever he might do. Very likely there would be turmoil in the enemy camp, with recriminations and so forth.

Well, that would be all to the good. With placid satisfaction supplanted by doubt and apprehension, some frantic and ill-judged moves might be expected in the place of careful planning, with meticulous attention to details. And lack of attention to seemingly insignificant details often proved the downfall of just such an outfit. Coming on the heels of the merciless beating inflicted on two of their number and their subse-quent death in the course of the frustrated widelooping attempt, which immediately followed the death of the three killers who took part in Bruff Carter's murder, the unexpected development could create downright consternation. At least Slade hoped so.

Not that he would be relieved of personal danger. The bunch was in too deep to pull back. One more killing, even of a peace officer, wouldn't matter; you can stretch a rope just so far. He would have to be even more vigilant if he wished to stay alive. He wondered in what manner the next attempt would come. Something subtle, perhaps, seeing as they hadn't had much luck with direct methods. To heck with it! Worry about it when the time came, when it would be too late, one way or the other, to worry. So he wouldn't worry at all.

The orchestra put in an appearance, the dance floor girls following. Slade was relieved to see Yolanda among them. He caught her eye and waved. She smiled and waved back.

"A nice gal," observed Watkins. "I knew her dad well, Henry Murdock. He had a little feed store over on Losoya Street, but went busted. Died soon afterward and the gal had to go to work. Mother already dead. Guess she can make more money dancing than at anything else she might know how to do. Floor dancing is all right in a nice place like this. Norm Allen don't stand for no foolishness."

"Allen a native of San Antonio?" Slade asked idly.

"Nope," Watkins replied. "Don't know just where he came from. Showed up here something over a year back and bought the Calaorra. It's an old line place—been on this corner for years—but was sort of going to seed when Allen took over. He changed all that and made an up and coming place of it. Everything strictly on the square. A nice quiet feller, Allen. I've a notion he was a big city man once; the sort of drinks he introduced here makes me think so. Talks like a pretty well educated *hombre*. A plumb gentleman, all right, but he can be salty if necessary. Quick as a cat on his feet and hits like the kick of a mule. Mighty fast with that shoulder gun he wears, too. I saw him pull on a feller who had his iron already out; Allen shot first and plugged the obstreperous gent through the arm. Reckon he could just as easy killed him if he'd been a mind to. Well, let's have a drink and then I'll have to get back to the store and help close up for the day. I always like to drink with law officers."

"I'm not a law officer yet," Slade smiled.

"Don't worry, you will be," Watkins declared with confidence as he raised his glass. "Here's to your deputy's badge. Gotta go. Be seeing you."

He hurried to the door, glancing at his watch. Slade turned and surveyed Norman Allen lounging gracefully at the end of the bar.

NINE

Finishing his drink, he strolled to the dance floor and had a dance with Yolanda.

"I missed you last night and wondered what had happened," she said. "Today I learned what did. What a violent life you lead, Mr. Slade."

"Not always," he replied. "I have my quiet moments."

"I've a notion they're few and far between," she returned. "Should have one if you remain here tonight. Quiet tonight. Always is the night before payday for the ranches. Be different tomorrow night. Wouldn't be surprised if we get off early tonight."

"I'll be here when you do," he promised.

While they were having a second dance, Sheriff Rader arrived and took a seat near the poker game. After the dance ended, Slade relinquished Yolanda to a laughing-eyed young cowhand and joined the sheriff. Rader jerked his thumb toward the poker game.

"Dawson's celebrating getting his cows back," he said. "If he drops the price of them in that game he won't pay it no mind, but he hates to have anything taken off him."

"Nobody likes to be robbed," Slade replied. "Get a good sleep?"

"Not as much as I needed," said the sheriff. "I'm going to bed early. Another inquest tomorrow afternoon, on those nine hellions we packed in. Just a waste of time, if you ask me, but the coroner thinks there should be one. Have a drink?"

Slade shook his head. "I think I'll walk around a bit and look things over," he said. "It's an interesting town."

"Too darn interesting at times," grunted Rader. "See you tomorrow."

"By the way, have you any notion where Norman Allen originally came from?" Slade asked as he stood up.

"Don't believe I ever heard him say," Rader replied. "From somewhere over east, I imagine. Perhaps Louisiana. Seems to me I remember him once saying something about dealing cards on the Mississippi boats. Not sure about it. Why?"

"I was just wondering," Slade answered. "He doesn't talk like a Texan. Be seeing you."

San Antonio was interesting and Slade spent several instructive hours walking the streets that radiated like a huge spider web from the irregular quadrilateral bounded by Houston and Commerce Streets, Alamo Plaza and Main Avenue.

He strolled along Dolorosa Street, so named because of the atrocities committed there by the Spanish General, Don Joaquin Arredondo, who imprisoned three hundred citizens in an airless building where eighteen smothered before the remainder were taken out and shot. Each day he forced the women to convert twenty-four bushels of corn into *tortillas* for his army and so mistreated them that the street which passed the place of imprisonment was known as the Street of Sorrow—*Dolorosa*, and so it remained.

He gazed at the crumbling, ivy-covered walls of the Alamo, the cradle of Texas liberty, where two hundred Texas patriots fought and died to the last man, their guns still grasped in their stiffened hands.

He seemed to hear the thunder of those Alamo guns, roaring defiance to overwhelming odds. Guns of the Alamo! They were silent now, those Guns of the Alamo that fought for liberty. But down through the years the guns of Texas soldiers and Texas peace officers had fought and were still fighting the never ending battle for liberty, law and justice. Guns of the Alamo—all!

He returned to the Calaorra, his spirit uplifted, where Yolanda, her night's work finished, awaited him.

As they walked along Commerce Street, Slade had an inspiration. "It's not so very late," he said. "How'd you like to drop into a place I discovered over on West Nueva Street?"

"Would suit me fine, I'm not sleepy," she replied. "Do you think it will still be open?"

"I don't think it ever closes," Slade replied with a laugh. "I'll wager we'll find it still going strong."

Slade was right. La Culebra was still going strong. Serge Kendricks, who spotted them as soon as they entered, came over and helped them find a table. His eyes seemed to blink a little as they rested on Yolanda's elfinly beautiful face. Slade performed the introductions.

"We thought we'd drop in for a nightcap," he added. "Won't you join us?"

Kendricks hesitated, glancing at Yolanda. "Please do, Mr. Kendricks," she seconded the invitation.

"I'll be glad to," he replied, dropping into a chair, "but you'll be my guests."

Despite his forbidding appearance, Kendricks proved to be an affable and charming host. Soon he and Yolanda were conversing animatedly. Slade sat mostly silent and listened.

He had not been altogether without guile in arranging the meeting. Men will often talk freely with a pretty woman, and Kendricks might inadvertently let drop something of significance.

But as he listened to the conversation, Slade's black brows drew together slightly. Kendricks was talking about his past, all right, but the way he portrayed it, it was certainly an innocuous past. He was telling her how he worked in a coal mine to get together enough money to finish high school and a year in college, where he studied navigation. Of his experiences on the sea, including the fight with the Lascar mutineers. Of how he had saved enough money to, when tired of the sea, buy the La Culebra saloon, which was paying well. He confided that his ambition was to acquire a small ranch and raise cattle, which he hoped to be able to do in a year or two. And so forth. And he had an interested listener.

Slade smiled to himself, a bit wryly. Looked like his little scheme had backfired a mite, as it were.

After quite a while, during which El Halcon was something in the nature of friendly spectator, Yolanda said,

"It's getting late. Really we must go."

"You'll come back?" Kendricks asked eagerly. "If Mr. Slade can't bring you, I'll come for you at the Calaorra, if I may."

"That would be fine," she answered. "Mr. Slade is a busy man and not always to be depended on."

Outside she remarked, "He's not a handsome man, but he's nice. I like him."

"You two seemed to get along well together," Slade said, with a smile.

She slanted him a sideways glance. "If one can't have the moon, it's not too bad to compromise for sixpence," she said.

Slade thought that one over and decided it was best not to comment. As a matter of fact, he was beset by certain qualms and a disquieting uneasiness. His little stratagem which had appeared innocuous enough when he formulated it, had burgeoned into a problem. Yolanda's reaction to Serge Kendricks had been unexpected, and surprising. Blast it! There was no foretelling what a woman would do or what would appeal to her. He liked Yolanda and didn't want her to get hurt. And he still hadn't made up his mind relative to Kendricks. Women! he lamented to himself. Why did he always have to get mixed up with them!

Not an original plaint, men having irritably asked themselves that question ever since Adam woke up and found himself short a rib.

He told her good night at her door and before retiring himself, headed for the livery stable and his nightly visit to Shadow. As he turned a corner and approached the mouth of the alley on which the stable stood, he heard a raucous voice break into ribald song. A moment later he saw the singer lurching and weaving down the street beyond the alley mouth. He chuckled. Evidently the gentleman had looked on the wine when it was red, doubtless in the form of straight whiskey. He turned into the alley and immediately stopped chuckling. From the gloomy depths came the sound of swift steps.

Instantly he was on the alert, but the steps faded away into the distance. Nevertheless he kept in the shadow as much as possible, hugging the walls of dark warehouses which flanked the alley on both sides. However, nothing happened and he neared the stable door, fumbling a key from his pocket, for the old stable keeper who slept above the stalls always kept the door locked, giving keys to patrons he considered trustworthy.

Slade was reaching the key toward the lock when abruptly he paused, staring at the door, which certainly should have been locked. It wasn't. A little light filtered from a street lamp on the corner and the faint gleam revealed to his keen eyes that the door stood slightly ajar, just an inch or so, but ajar.

Slipping the key back in his pocket, he stood listening, considering the situation. Of course the stable keeper might have neglected to snap the lock, but Slade thought that highly unlikely. Then why was it unlocked and slightly open? Some careless cowhand taking out his horse might have forgotten to close it. No, that also was unlikely. The keeper would have almost certainly been present when the animal was removed, and he would have made sure the door was not left open. Standing perfectly motionless, Slade listened for any sound within. Nothing broke the silence except the breathing of the horses and the occasional stamp of a nervous hoof.

Just the same, he didn't fancy the situation. Somebody could be in there waiting for him to appear outlined against the opening. The subtle sixth sense that develops in men who ride much alone with danger as a stirrup companion was warning him that all was not well, and he had learned not to disregard the promptings of that voiceless monitor.

Flattened against the wall beyond the door hinges, he slowly and carefully stretched out a long arm until he could reach the knob, closing his fingers about it, careful not to make the slightest sound. He got a firm grip and flung the door wide open.

There was a thunderous roar. Smoke and yellow flame gushed through the opening. Slade was hurled clean across the alley to thud against the opposite wall and fall in a heap.

Half dazed, blinded, his ears ringing like bells, he scrambled to his feet, hands streaking to his guns and stood weaving. The air was hideous with the screams of terrified horses. Upstairs the stable keeper was bellowing curses. Hugging the wall, Slade glanced in every direction, and saw nothing. He strode forward as light appeared inside the stable. The keeper, barefooted and in a long nightgown, was padding down the stairs, a lamp in one hand, a cocked sixgun in the other.

"What the blankety-blue blazes is going on here?" he bawled.

"Take it easy, everything appears to be under control," Slade called back.

The keeper held up the lamp. "Oh, it's you!" he exclaimed. "What the devil do you mean by kicking the door down at this time of night? Didn't I give you a key?"

"Yes, I guess you did," Slade replied. He was staring at where the door sill should have been. Instead, there was a hole in the ground. The door itself, split and splintered, was sagging crazily on one hinge.

The keeper also stared. "What—how—what—" he sputtered.

"Judging from the smell and the row it kicked up, I'd say it was dynamite," Slade replied. "You sure you locked that door last night?"

"Of course I'm sure," the keeper yelped, waving the gun, which was still at full cock.

"Put the hammer of that thing down before you blow another hole in the wall," Slade advised. "Well, the door wasn't locked when I got here. It was open a crack. I thought it didn't look just right and pulled it wide open without standing in line. Got blown clear across the alley as it was. If I'd been in line, I reckon I'd have landed in the next county."

The keeper raved curses. Slade called soothingly to the frightened horses and examined the damage done.

"Guess the hellion must have wedged the stick against the sill and couldn't quite close the door," he announced. "Was evidently triggered with some sort of a device to slam the cap when the door was opened wide. Yes, here's a bit of wire still hanging to the inside knob. Ingenious, and lethal."

"But why would anybody do such a thing?" demanded the keeper.

"That's your question, and you know the section better than I do," Slade replied evasively.

Shouts were sounding in the distance, drawing

nearer. Evidently the explosion had been heard by others.

"Let's try and close the door," Slade suggested. "Otherwise half the town is liable to be boiling in here asking questions we can't answer. No need of that."

"Right," growled the keeper, lending a hand. Between them they got the door closed. A moment later they heard a voice call.

"Sounded like it was around here somewhere, but I don't see anything busted up."

Other voices sounded, a confused murmur that gradually stilled away. Slade made sure none of the horses, including Shadow, had suffered injury and came back to the keeper who had donned boots and was stuffing a pipe with tobacco. Slade sat down on the lowest step of the stairs and rolled a cigarette.

"Who in heck could the sidewinder have been after?" wondered the keeper.

"Hard to tell," Slade replied. "Looks like somebody has a grudge against somebody. Guess you'll have a little chore of carpentering on your hands."

"And some work with a spade to fill that hole," the other grunted. "I wish I'd be using it to dig a hole to plant the hellion in."

While the keeper appraised the damage done to his door, Slade sat smoking and thinking. Well, he had his answer as to how the "next" attempt would be made. Subtle, all right, and clever, with allowances made against any chance of it misfiring. Evidently he was being kept closely under surveillance. His nightly pilgrimages to the stable had been noted. The supposedly inebriated hellion had been stationed at the alley mouth to notify his confederate at the stable door of his approach. When he saw him round the corner, a burst of maudlin song had been the signal. Then the other had quickly placed his lethal contrivance and decamped down the alley.

Yes, very clever, and only his habitual caution and his penchant for not overlooking any suspicious detail no matter how insignificant had saved him from being blown to kingdom come. Well, doubtless there would be more; he'd have to be continually on his guard. However, that wasn't anything new for El Halcon. He bestowed a final pat on Shadow.

"Yes, you might as well notify the sheriff of what happened, if you're of a mind to," he told the stable keeper. "Not that it'll likely do any good. Okay, if you've decided not, I'll keep a tight latigo on my jaw, and we'll keep the hellion guessing. And it might not be good for business for this to get around. Good night, I'm heading for bed."

He walked warily to the hotel, although he hardly expected any more excitement for the time being.

"Getting to be a regular night owl," he grumbled as he undressed. "Never see the sun rise any more. Guess this city life isn't for me; too darn hectic."

TEN

Payday! The streets were filled with cowboys and ranch owners, all set for a rarin' bust; for San Antonio was, and is, a veritable cattle capital. The mesquite covered acres stretch almost endlessly south and west. Winter vegetables, fruits, berries, cotton, wool, mohair, and oil were coming to the fore, but the lusty business of the open range was still the predominant factor in the town's economic life. Since immediately after the Civil War the great cattle drives had rolled north, and San Antonio was in their path. San Antonio boasted a turbulent past, an equally turbulent present, and looked forward, without error, to a turbulent future. Its streets follow trails beaten by mustangs and cattle drives, and before those the moccasined feet of Indians. Violent deeds and vivid episodes splash its history. Again and again armies fought for the city, won victories, suffered defeats, and vanished down the corridor of the years; but San Antonio remained.

All this Slade reviewed in his mind as he sauntered toward the Calaorra for some breakfast. His pessimism of the dark hours had dissipated with the sun and he looked forward eagerly to forthcoming events.

He decided, however, that before eating he

would drop in at the sheriff's office to get the low-down on the inquest. He found Rader in a bad temper.

"She's liable to be a heller before the night's over," he predicted. "I can feel it in the air. I've sworn in some specials I can depend on to keep an eye on things. I smell trouble."

San Antonio boasted a town marshal and a police force of sorts, but the rugged old frontier peace officer looked upon these as little better than expensive ornaments, not always so ornamental, of inefficient municipal government.

"Let something really bad bust loose and they'll come yelling to me for help," he declared. "Those city dudes ain't good for nothing except to pull in somebody for spitting on the sidewalk."

"The marshal doesn't look so bad," Slade remarked. "I saw him the other night, giving me the once-over without approval."

"He can stand a lot of improvement," grunted Rader. "Oh, well, I suppose those jiggers have to eat, too. Which reminds me, I ain't had any breakfast. Suppose we go get some; the inquest isn't till two this afternoon."

They found the Calaorra already fairly crowded, mostly with cowhands. The sheriff eyed them with cold disapproval.

"They'll start something, see if they don't," he said. "And that La Culebra rumhole we visited the other night. I expect that to blow sky high before morning. Which reminds me, some fellers told me they heard a dynamite explosion somewhere around last night. Did you happen to hear it?"

"Yes, I heard it, and felt it," Slade replied.

The sheriff stared. "What the devil do you mean by that?" he demanded.

Slade told him, in detail. The sheriff did some fancy swearing.

"So they tried again, eh?" he growled.

"Looked sort of that way," Slade conceded. "I told the stable keeper to forget it. Didn't see any sense in spreading it around. Let the devils puzzle over how it misfired."

"They'll puzzle, all right, but they won't give up," predicted the sheriff. "Here comes the chuck; let's eat."

Followed a period of busy silence, food being more important to hungry men than conversation. It was broken by the sheriff mumbling through a mouthful of egg.

"Here comes Will Dawson looking like a cat that's just lapped up a saucer of cream and sees the canary's cage door open." He gestured to a chair, to which Dawson dropped, his black eyes snapping.

"Yesterday was my lucky day," he announced. "Got my two hundred cows back and won two hundred pesos at poker." He drew forth a roll of bills and began riffling them.

"What say, Slade," he said familiarly, "we'll

divvy. You got something coming for getting those cows back."

Slade smilingly shook his head. "Got a few pesos laid aside, but thank you just the same," he replied.

"Never saw such a feller—you can't do anything for him!" wailed Dawson. "Maybe you might like to sign up with me on the spread," he added hopefully. "Be nice to have you around singing to the cows. If you do, I'll bed down with the herd."

"Might not be a bad notion, some time," Slade avoided a direct answer. "Your boys going to be in town for the bust?"

"Couldn't keep 'em away with a battery of shotguns," Dawson replied, putting up his money. "Yep, they'll all be here. I'll have to keep an eye on the hellions; they'll be rarin' to go when the redeye starts buzzin' in their ears. Hello, Norm, send me a drink before I order a surroundin'."

"With pleasure, Mr. Dawson," Norman Allen, who had approached, replied. "Waiter, a round on the house. How are you, Mr. Slade? Everybody is singing your praises."

"They'd ought to be," growled Dawson. "If he'll just stick around a spell and keep on the way he's been doing, he'll have this blasted town cleaned up till it's peaceful as an old maid's picnic."

"I've a feeling you wouldn't particularly care for it if it were too peaceful," Allen said with a smile. "You'd very likely go hunting for some place not so quiet."

"Oh, I like excitement, all right, but I don't go for thievin' and snake-blooded killings," Dawson answered. "Those I can do without, and we've had too much of 'em hereabouts of late."

Allen smiled again. "As the Scriptures say of the poor, those we will always have with us," he remarked and strolled back to the bar.

"I can't make that feller out," complained Dawson. "He talks in riddles."

"He's a good deal of a riddle himself," observed the sheriff. "Will talk about anything except himself. Never says a word about himself. Always pleasant and smiling, but down at the bottom he's a cold proposition or I miss my guess. Tell you about something that happened not long after he took over this place. They were just getting ready to close up and there was nobody here but Norm and Bruff Carter behind the bar. Norm was sitting at the bar counting the day's take, which was plenty, I guess. Carter told me about it."

The sheriff paused to take a swallow of coffee, then resumed:

"A feller walked in and up to the bar. Bruff said all of a sudden he stopped dead still, stared at Norm and went for his gun. Norm beat him to the draw and plugged him between the eyes. Bruff figured, and so did everybody else, that the feller aimed to hold up the joint for the take. Guess he did, but he picked on the wrong jigger."

"What did Norm say?" asked Dawson.

"Said he supposed that was what the feller meant to do. Said he didn't wait to find out and didn't take any chances when he saw that iron coming out. Said he never saw the feller before, so he'd hardly have any other reason for pulling on him."

"Nobody know who the feller was?" Dawson questioned.

"Yep, somebody recognized him," Rader replied. "Said his name was Jack Richardson and that he used to be one of King Fisher's bunch before Fisher was killed right down the street from here. Guess he had a hold-up in mind, all right."

"King Fisher's men were salty hombres," observed Dawson.

"Some of the worst that ever came out of Texas," nodded the sheriff.

Slade gazed at Norman Allen lounging against the bar, and his eyes were thoughtful. The name Jack Richardson was familiar to him. Ranger records rated him a gambler and a killer whose gun was for hire, but never as a robber.

Sheriff Rader looked at his watch. "Well, if you've finished eating, Will, I reckon we'd better amble over to the inquest," he said. "Getting close to two o'clock. Waste of time, as I said before, but I guess the coroner figures he'd oughta do something to earn his pay."

The inquest took even less time than the one held on Bruff Carter. Slade, Sheriff Rader and everybody who took part in the affair in which the wideloopers met their death were credited with having done a good chore. Several jurymen shook hands with Slade.

"Keep up the good work, feller," one oldtimer remarked. "Fellers like you and Wyatt Earp and John Slaughter are what this section needs. Hot lead is the only thing those hellions can understand. Some of us fellers were figuring to write Jinx McNelty for some Rangers, but I'm beginning to think that won't be necessary."

After the inquest, Slade walked the streets for some time. He dropped into many places, studying the crowd, listening to snatches of conversation. Everywhere he found turbulence and hilarity but, so far as he could see, nothing sinister; but the day was still young and most anything could happen before the night was over.

On the Navarra Street bridge he paused and leaned on the railing, gazing down at the smoothly flowing water of the river, his black brows drawing together. He couldn't get the sheriff's story of the killing of Jack Richardson out of his mind. The Ranger dossier of questionable characters, which Slade had studied many times, listed Richardson as, setting aside the redoubtable King Fisher himself, having the fastest and deadliest gun hand of all the King Fisher outfit. Norman Allen must be mighty good with a gun to have shaded Richardson.

However, Slade knew it is not always the fastest gun that comes out on top. If his first shot misses and that of his adversary who is not so fast on the pull but gets set and shoots accurately does not, speed doesn't do him much good. Slade wondered if Richardson had managed to pull trigger before he was downed. The sheriff hadn't mentioned that he had and the intimation was that he had not; he'd check that with Rader.

Also, any little slip will slow up a draw, the hammer catching on an article of clothing, the sight dragging against the holster, a sweaty hand. All such possibilities have to be reckoned with by the man who reaches, and if one occurs he's very likely on the short end of the deal.

No, the race was not always to the swift; the famous Wyatt Earp, who never felt the burn of lead, always got set before he pulled trigger, and didn't miss. The same applied to John Ringo, Curly Bill Brocius and other outstanding artists with a Colt. Now and then there was a man who was extremely fast and lethally accurate at the same time, himself for instance, but he was the exception not the rule. Norman Allen might be in either category. But why was he devoting so much conjecture to Allen? His thoughts turned to La Culebra and its enigmatic owner; he'd drop in there later.

The sun had set. The river was flaming purple, the shattered walls of the Alamo vibrant with color. The low western hills were washed in pale gold. Overhead the sky was rose and scarlet and tremulous violet. The empty eyes of windows were bursting forth as rectangles of orange, the street lights blooming pale flowers that soon would burgeon to amber blossoms on the black robe of the night. Slade descended from the comb of the bridge and walked slowly through the deepening twilight to where the busy streets of San Antonio boomed with lusty life. His pulse quickened, although the scene of beauty he had just witnessed was sharply contrasted by the hectic activity that while stimulating was not always beautiful. Feeling hungry, he entered the Calaorra and by good luck found a small unoccupied table in a corner.

For now the Calaorra was really booming. Men lined the bar three deep. Several card games were in progress. The roulette wheels were spinning, the faro bank going strong. The dance floor was so crowded that the dancers could do little more than shuffle. The condition, however, gave their partners excuse to hold the girls close, and the girls didn't seem to mind. Slade chuckled and gave his order to a waiter.

As he waited to be served, Yolanda disengaged

herself from the prairie dog tangle on the floor and joined him. Her eyes were bright, her cheeks flushed, her lips vividly red.

"Whe-e-ew!" she exclaimed as she dropped into the chair Slade pulled out for her. "It's fun, but hard on the toes. They've been walked on more than I've used them for walking."

Slade ordered a bottle of wine, which would give her an excuse to sit out a couple of dances. He filled her glass and she sipped daintily.

"I don't drink much," she said, "but I'm warm and this tastes good."

"Your complexion attests to the fact that you don't," he replied.

She smiled at him, showing a dimple at one corner of her sweetly shaped mouth. Slade reproached himself for not having noticed it before.

"Looks like it's going to be a big night," he observed.

"Yes," she agreed. "Payday nights always are, but this one seems more than average. Wonder how La Culebra is making out?"

"Chances are it's hopping like a hen on hot plates," he answered. "I figure to drop in there later. Wouldn't be surprised if Serge Kendricks ambles in here before the night is over."

"He said he would," she replied. "We girls can leave the floor at four in the morning if we wish."

"I'd think that would be enough of it," he said. "Have something to eat with your drinks?"

She shook her head. "I ate before going on the floor," she replied. "Hardly expected to get a chance to afterward. Here comes Mr. Allen."

The proprietor approached, smiling genially. "Howdy, Mr. Slade?" he greeted. "Will Dawson left word that he'd be in later and hoped to see you."

"I'll stick around till he shows up," Slade promised. "You're doing a business tonight."

"Yes," Allen nodded, "but I wish it were over. Everything okay so far, but a gathering like this is always productive of trouble. A wild bunch in here."

"No harm in most of them," Slade commented. "Rowdy and boisterous, but that's about all."

"Yes, but there's always an element watching for a chance to turn an illicit profit," Allen returned morosely. "Town's getting big, too, and you can't know everybody. An advantage to a small community; there you know who to watch out for. Bad for business if somebody is robbed or hurt after leaving here. I have three extra floor men on the job to put down any trouble that starts in here, but I can't police the streets. Be seeing you; I'll send over a drink."

"He seems worried and nervous of late," Yolanda observed. "Snappy with the help, which he never used to be. Acts as if something is bothering him."

"This business is not productive of tranquillity," Slade answered.

"That's what Serge says," she remarked. "That's why he wants to get into the cattle business where he'll have peace."

"That also has its moments," Slade smiled. "But I've a notion he'll be better satisfied looking at cows' tails instead of up-ended whiskey glasses."

"I think so, too," she said. "Well, I'll have to be getting back to the floor. Please try and take care of yourself."

ELEVEN

Dawson did not appear while Slade was eating, but Sheriff Rader did.

"Nothing serious so far," he remarked. "Guess the dudes in their fancy suits are doing a better job than I expected; but the night's young. Figure to visit the Nueva Street rum-hole later. If anything busts loose, it'll be there. What have you made up your mind to about the scar-faced hellion who runs it?"

"I'm not completely sure just yet," Slade replied. "But I'm beginning to fear that you're barking up the wrong tree and that the coon's roosting elsewhere."

"What makes you say that?" asked the sheriff.

"I don't know," Slade admitted frankly. "The man's general attitude, perhaps. For one thing, I don't credit him with the kind of brains neces-|sary to handle such a bunch as is working out here."

"He always looks bad to me," grunted Rader.

"A Ranger learns not to put much trust in outward appearances," Slade said. "Contrary to popular opinion, bad men don't run to a pattern. I've known some who appeared to be honest and upright gentlemen, and weren't. You may have heard that John Wesley Hardin, about the worst

116

that ever came out of Texas, was often mistaken for a minister. He did start off teaching school."

"But if we discard Kendricks as a suspect, who the devil have we got?" demanded Rader.

"That's your question, and if you haven't the answer, I'm sure I haven't," Slade countered.

"Then you have no notion as to who to look for?"

Slade hesitated. "I'm evolving a nebulous theory with nothing concrete on which to base it," he said slowly. "Something in the nature of a hunch, if you believe in hunches. Really it's little more than a feeling, but I've experienced that sort of feeling before and learned not to altogether disregard it. Seems ridiculous on the face of it, but you never can tell. I've gotten some surprises in my time."

"I hope you get one this time, of the right sort," growled the sheriff. "Got no more to say about it?"

"Not at present," Slade replied. "For I may be shooting wide of the mark. "I wish to be a lot surer than I am now before I do any talking."

"I see," nodded the sheriff. "Oh, heck! Let's go over to La Culebra."

Leaving the main business section behind, they walked along Nueva Street and crossed the creek.

"Good to get a breath of fresh air," grunted Rader.

"Yes, it's quieter over here," Slade agreed.

117

"You wait!" predicted the sheriff.

La Culebra was not quiet. It was jam-packed to the doors with hilarious humanity. Slade quickly decided, however, that despite the noise the gathering was fairly innocuous.

With difficulty, Serge Kendricks made room for them at the end of the bar.

"A few more nights like this and I'll have my cow factory," he chuckled.

"Or nervous prostration," Slade smiled.

"Oh, I rather like it, so long as there's no trouble," Kendricks said. "The boys are having a good time and after a month of hard work I reckon they deserve it."

Sheriff Rader wandered off in search of the lavatory. Kendricks turned to Slade.

"How is it in—the other places?" he asked.

"About the same as here, although I think you have the biggest crowd I've noticed so far," Slade answered. "Going to be at the Calaorra later?"

"I—I thought I might drop in for a minute," Kendricks hesitated.

"You're expected," Slade said, the little devils of laughter dancing in the back of his eyes.

Hendricks flushed. "She's a darned nice girl," he mumbled.

"She's all of that," Slade agreed. "I'm glad to see her getting a break."

Kendricks regarded him curiously. "You don't mind?"

118

"Not in the least," Slade assured him. "The best of luck to you both."

"Funny she'd be willing to take up with a jigger with a map like I've got. I can't hardly believe t," Kendricks said, a little sadly.

Slade's steady eyes were abruptly all kindness. "Serge," he said, "I'm not very old and I've got a lot to learn about women, but this much I have learned: the right sort don't put too much stock in outward appearances. They have a way of looking inside a man and seeing what's really there, and if it looks right to them, that's all that counts."

"I hope you're right," Kendricks sighed. "I wouldn't want her to be unhappy." Slade saw that there were tears in his eyes.

"She won't be," he predicted, and meant it.

And he knew he was due to tell Sheriff Rader to just forget all about Serge Kendricks and concentrate on dropping a loop on the side-winder who really *was* responsible for the hell raising in the section.

When the old peace officer returned to the bar, Slade and Kendricks were having a drink together, and Slade's hand rested on the latter's shoulder.

Sheriff Rader could see farther into the trunk of a tree than most. "Well, I'll be hanged!" he muttered.

"So you've made up your mind about him,

eh?" he remarked when Kendricks hurried off to attend to a chore.

"Yep," Slade replied cheerfully. "We'll waste a little time here—the place is interesting—and then go trail hunting again. Here's hoping we have some luck."

On their way back to the Calaorra they stopped at a number of places and found everything under control. There had been a few tussles here and there but nothing really serious.

"Better than I'd hoped for," said the sheriff. "You never can tell. A hullabaloo like this and nothing happens. What's supposed to be a quiet night and all heck busts loose. No, you never can tell about a cow country crowd; always coming up with surprises. Looks like we might get through the night without any real trouble. I hope so."

At the Calaorra they found Will Dawson standing talking with Allen in a quiet spot near the wall. He waved them to join him.

"Was wanting to ask you to drop over to my *casa* when you have time, Slade," he said. "I'd like to talk to you about something. Like to show you over my holding. Might even persuade you to sing for me. What do you say?"

"I will," Slade promised. "Tomorrow. Today, rather, it's well past midnight."

"Fine!" said Dawson. "Well, I see a vacant chair at the poker game over there; guess I'll look at a few hands. Had enough to drink for one night."

120

Slade and the sheriff found a vacant table after a while and ordered coffee. Finally Rader looked at his watch.

"I'm going over to the office and drowse in my chair," he said. "If anything busts loose I reckon I'll hear about it."

"The way things look, you might as well go to bed," Slade replied. "I think I'll stick around for a while."

Rader got up and lumbered out. Slade sat sipping coffee and smoking. Tired nature was taking toll and the crowd was beginning to thin out. Yolanda caught his eye, glanced at the clock over the bar and nodded.

It was not quite four when Serge Kendricks entered, spotted Slade and joined him. Slade saw Norman Allen staring at him curiously, as did the men with whom he was talking. However, he did not come over to greet the La Culebra owner.

At precisely four o'clock, Yolanda left the dance floor and sat down at the table. Slade noted that again curious glances were bent their way from the end of the bar; heads drew together there.

Kendricks ordered wine for Yolanda, whiskey for himself. Slade took more coffee. The three men who had been talking with Norman Allen at the end of the bar left the saloon. Allen stayed where he was.

Presently Kendricks suggested, "After we have another drink, how'd you like to go over to my place for a while? Still lively there."

"I'd love to," Yolanda replied.

Slade abruptly decided to play a hunch. "I'll see you there later," he said. "I'm going out and walk around a while."

Leaving the Calaorra, he walked to North Main Street, then turned south till he reached West Nueva, where he turned west. Sauntering along, he made sure he was not followed. Reaching South Flores Street, he walked north a few paces, leaned against a building wall and waited.

Presently he saw Kendricks and Yolanda approaching on Nueva from the east, arm in arm, talking together. He waited until they had passed and were some distance ahead, then followed. Before reaching the bridge across San Pedro Creek he lengthened his stride and began closing the distance. The pair were so engrossed in each other that they never turned their heads and not until he was less than a dozen paces to the rear did he slow down.

Beyond the bridge the lighting was even poorer. Slade moved a little closer. Ahead yawned a dark alley mouth.

Kendricks and Yolanda passed the alley, heads close together. From the black mouth a man glided. Slade saw the gleam of the knife raised to strike. He drew and shot.

The knife wielder crumpled up like a sack of old clothes. His steel tinkled to the ground.

A gun blazed from the alley mouth. The slug grained Slade's ribs and knocked him sideways with the shock. Shooting with both hands, he sprayed the alley mouth with lead. Weaving and ducking, he raced forward. The shots were not answered.

Kendricks had whirled around, a gun in his hand, looking badly startled and very bewildered. Yolanda cowered against him.

"Stay where you are!" Slade snapped. He peered into the alley, thought he heard the beat of feet somewhere in the distance. He took a long stride forward, and plunged onto his face.

TWELVE

Yolanda screamed. Kendricks gave a yelp of dismay. Slade scrambled to his feet, saying things under his breath that were not fitting to a lady's ears.

"What happened? Kendricks called anxiously as he started to Slade's aid.

"Stay where you are," the Ranger repeated. "Smart hellions stretched a rope across the alley to trip anybody who might try to chase them; it worked. Stay where you are."

He explored the alley for some distance, zigzagging back and forth, and found nothing. Ejecting the spent shells from his guns and replacing them with fresh cartridges, he returned to where Kendricks and Yolanda waited.

"The sidewinder kept going," he said, holstering his guns. "Guess I missed him."

"Slade, what in blazes is it all about?" demanded the bewildered saloonkeeper.

El Halcon gestured to the long knife glinting evilly in the dim light.

"Jigger appeared to want to try the edge of his sticker on your backbone," he replied. "I had to take an awful chance with you two right in line, but if I hadn't, you'd have gotten that steel between your shoulder blades. Nice people!"

124

Yolanda whimpered and clutched Kendricks' arm. "I—I guess I'm just a bad luck piece," she sobbed.

"Oh, no, you're not," Slade said. "Except that you're so darned attractive when a man's beside you he forgets everything else."

The big eyes slanted toward him. "You didn't," she said pointedly.

"Perhaps more than you think," Slade smiled. "Keep your ears open, now, and let me know if you hear anybody coming. I want to look this hellion over. Chances are if the shots were heard they were put down as just some cowhands skylarking like they've been doing all night, but keep your ears open."

Squatting on his heels, he peered at the dead face. It was a rather scrubby-looking face, the forehead low, the nose fleshy at the base, the mouth loose, the chin retreating. The only outstanding feature of the unsavory countenance was a wide, jagged scar stretching from the left corner of the mouth almost to the ear and gleaming white against the fellow's swarthy skin.

"Border scum!" he muttered to himself. "The sort that will kill for a couple of pesos." He beckoned Kendricks and Yolanda.

"I'm going to strike a match," he said. "I want you to take a good look at this hellion and tell me if you've seen him before."

A moment later Kendricks shook his head. "But

I have," the girl exclaimed. "Last night in the Calaorra. That scar! He was talking with some men at the end of the bar."

"Do you recall the men?" Slade asked quickly. She shook her head.

"I hardly noticed them," she replied. "I wouldn't have noticed him had it not been for the scar. I thought it looked terrible."

Slade nodded and began turning out the contents of the fellow's pockets.

Nothing of significance was revealed except a surprisingly large sum of money, which he replaced.

"The price of murder," he remarked to Kendricks. "Looks like you come rather high."

"Please don't joke about it," begged Yolanda. "I feel terrible!"

"But everything turned out okay, thanks to Slade," Kendricks comforted her.

The fellow wore rather shabby and ordinary town clothes. Under his coat was a shoulder holster. Slade drew the gun and glanced at it.

"Regulation Forty-five and not new," he said. Shoving it back into the holster, he stood up.

"Let's go," he said. "I'll report the incident to the sheriff and let him dispose of the carcass. Now, Kendricks," he added as they started walking away, "I want you to give me a straight answer. Have you any idea why this attempt was made on your life?"

"Yes," the saloonkeeper replied. "Yes, I have a notion. Recently I was approached by a couple of hellions who said they were from the syndicate—ever hear of it?"

"Yes, I've heard of it," Slade answered. "Go on."

"Well, they demanded a cut in the take," Kendricks resumed. "Said it would be good for my business, and my health if I agreed. I handed them about the best thrashing they ever got and kicked them out. Nothing happened, until tonight."

"And, I gather, nothing happened to Bruff Carter until quite a while after he had the run-in with them," Slade remarked thoughtfully. "A coldly calculating bunch; wait until their intended victim is lulled into a sense of false security. All right, forget it for the time being, but keep your eyes open hereafter."

"I will," Kendricks promised fervently. "I've got the shakes."

"They seem to specialize in knives, which is rather unusual for this section," Slade remarked musingly. "Well, a knife is quiet and it leaves a somewhat messy corpse as a warning to others. Somehow a knife victim looks worse than one that has stopped a slug. Something disconcerting about a knife handle protruding from between a person's shoulder blades."

"Please!" exclaimed Yolanda.

Slade chuckled. "Okay," he said. "I'll tighten the latigo on my jaw."

As they passed under a street light, Yolanda gave a little cry.

"Your shirt! It's torn, and there's blood on it. You're hurt!"

"Just a scratch where the slug skipped along my ribs," Slade deprecated the wound.

"Scratch or no, you'll have it attended to when we reach Serge's place," said Yolanda. "Now shut up and don't argue with me. Men are all alike when it comes to taking care of themselves. Dad was just the same."

Slade grinned at Kendricks. "See what you're going to be up against?"

"He needs someone to look after him," Yolanda broke in vigorously. "Look at that shirt! He put it on without having it ironed!"

"I was in a hurry and didn't notice," Kendricks explained sheepishly. Yolanda sniffed her disdain.

"Here we are," she said. "Listen to the noise! Right into the back room with you, Walt. Serge, take care of him."

Passing through the saloon, where the general hilarity appeared to have in no wise abated, they reached the back room, where Slade stripped off his shirt.

Kendricks examined the slight furrow along his ribs and pronounced it nothing to worry about.

"I've got some good salve and bandages and stickin' plaster," he said. "Always keep 'em handy to patch up gents who have differences of opinion. Getting to be a pretty good sawbones. I'll strap you up—bleeding's already stopped—and you'll be okay in a few days. But if it had landed a couple of inches to the right, you'd be over there along with that knifing devil."

"I deserved to get shot in payment for my own stupidity," Slade growled. "I might have known there'd be more than one of the hellions and kept moving. Instead, I stood right there in the light and gave him a fair target. Guess in his flurry over what happened he shot a mite too fast instead of lining sights properly. Yes, I sure asked for it."

"A man can't think of everything, especially at such a moment," Kendricks replied. "Anyhow, you sure saved my bacon, and I won't forget it. Anytime I get a chance to pay off the score I'll be right there with bells on. Okay, that should do it. Let's go out and get a drink; I feel the need of one."

"Coffee for me, if you don't mind," Slade said. "I can stand a sizeable helping of that."

"Me, too," Yolanda said. "I'm still shaking."

"How come you were so handy on the job at just the right moment?" Kendricks asked Slade.

"I played a hunch," the Ranger explained. "The set-up was much the same as the night Bruff Carter was murdered. I've learned that such outfits as we're up against usually follow a pattern of method, which often constitutes a weakness.

Find out how they operate and it's possible, to an extent, to guard against it. So I played a hunch that, having very likely watched your movements all night, they'd take advantage of what looked like opportunity due to your undoubted preoccupation with your company. Looks like the hunch was a straight one."

"It sure was," said Kendricks. "And it was sure to my advantage that you played it."

Slade did not mention, at the moment, the three men who quietly left the Calaorra just a few minutes before Kendricks did. For after all it was more than possible that they had nothing to do with the attempted killing.

All in all, Slade felt that, aside from eliminating some unsavory and minor members of the outfit, he was getting exactly nowhere. At least, however, he had a possible suspect, although not one iota of proof against him. And he had to admit that he might be shooting wide of the mark. Just some little things that appeared to tie up, but a great deal of Walt Slade's outstanding success as a Ranger was his penchant for noticing little things and his ability to weave them into a definite pattern. Right now there were too many loose threads banging around and nothing concrete about which to loop the ends. About all he had was a vague suspicion based on some dubious incidents and anecdotes that might well be explained by coincidence. However,

130

Slade did not put much faith in coincidence, for coincidence, so called, usually has a simple explanation once all the facts are available. Well, he'd keep on digging; maybe he'd strike paydirt.

With the gray of morning the crowd finally began to thin out. Slade stifled a yawn with his hand and turned to Kendricks.

"I'm going to bed," he announced, "but before I go I want to give you a little good advice: from now on don't go walking around alone after dark, not until this mess is cleaned up. I think you're safe enough in the daytime, but not at night. The outfit working hereabouts does so by way of fear engendered by quick vengeance on anybody who bucks them. You bucked them, and if they don't even the score, just so much of their grip on others is lost, which they can't afford if they hope to stay in business. So I figure they'll make another try for you if you give them anything in the shape of an opportunity. So if you are out at night, for any reason at all, even to meet Yolanda, have one of your floor men with you. Two would be even better, if you want to stay alive."

"He won't forget, that I'll promise you," put in Yolanda.

"No, I won't forget," Kendricks agreed. "The way you talk makes me feel creepy."

"Keep on feeling creepy and—stay alive," Slade said. "Be seeing you, it's almost daylight. Don't forget. And keep your eyes open."

Slade followed his own advice and kept *his* eyes very much open, along with his other faculties, daylight or no daylight. He wondered if the body of the slain drygulcher had been spirited away as had those implicated in the killing of Bruff Carter.

It hadn't. It was right where he left it, no pretty picture in the strengthening light. Apparently the other members of the outfit to which the hellion belonged had either considered attempting to retrieve it too risky or just didn't give a hang about it. A casual passerby would quite likely have given it a wide berth. Being caught too near a body in San Antonio's streets might lay one open to implications if nothing worse. He gazed at the distorted face a moment and passed on. Let the sheriff puzzle about it for a while, when its presence was reported to him, as it would be sooner or later.

THIRTEEN

Despite the fact that it was broad daylight before he went to sleep, Slade was up before noon. His first stop was the sheriff's office where he found Rader at his desk. The old peace officer regarded him from under his bushy brows.

"Well," he said, "were you responsible?"

"Responsible for what?" Slade countered.

"For the scar-faced jigger picked up near an alley mouth over on Nueva Street, plugged dead center, and the other one found about a block away with two holes in him. He evidently bled to death. Managed to amble a bit after he was shot. We found some blood spots in the alley. The town marshal, who never makes mistakes, of course, 'lowed they had gunned each other."

"Did you find anything else?" Slade asked.

"Yep," replied the sheriff, drawing a long-bladed knife from a drawer, "this sticker. Wonder who that was meant for? Found it alongside the scar-faced one; the marshal didn't notice it, but I did and brought it along for a souvenir. Incidentally, the scar-faced one was plugged in the back. I figure he was about to use the sticker on somebody when the slug stopped him."

"Very good deduction," Slade smiled, and proceeded to regale Rader with an account of what happened.

The sheriff nodded and did not appear particularly surprised. "So they're after Kendricks, too, eh?"

"They're after anybody who has the guts to buck them," Slade replied grimly. "Kendricks did, and he wasn't very gentle about it. He's got to watch his step from now on, but I figure he's pretty well equipped to take care of himself now that he is on his guard."

"And you'd better watch your step, too," counselled Rader. "You must have them rarin' and chargin' and mighty jumpy. Incidentally, the marshal found the rope stretched across the alley; fell over it."

Slade chuckled but did not comment. There was seldom any love lost between the old frontier peace officers, usually graduated from the range, and their town counterparts, who were mostly city men.

"And now what?" Rader asked.

"Now," Slade replied, "as soon as I have some breakfast I'm going to ride over to the Triangle D *casa* for a little visit with Will Dawson. He invited me, you'll remember, and I promised I would today. I'm not used to being cooped up in a town this way and feel the need of a little fresh air, and Shadow needs to stretch his legs."

"A good notion," agreed the sheriff, "I know how you feel. Only, watch your step."

"I will," Slade promised. "I've a notion the range is safer than anyplace else."

"Maybe," the sheriff was dubious. "The way things have been going hereabouts of late, I figure no place is safe any more."

Slade ate a leisurely breakfast and smoked a couple of cigarettes before heading for the livery stable and Shadow. There he found the old keeper pottering about and pausing from time to time to regard his repaired door with satisfaction.

"Good as new," he said. "Fact is, it needed a little patching before that dynamiting hellion busted it. Everything quiet here last night. I slept with one eye open but didn't need to. Going to take a ride?"

"Yes, over to Will Dawson's place," Slade replied.

"Fine feller, Dawson," said the keeper. "Knowed him for the past thirty years, ever since he was a young feller. Got a nice holding over there. Good man to work for. Would be to your advantage to sign up with him."

"You may have something there," Slade agreed and proceeded to get the rig on Shadow.

As soon as he was clear of the town, he sent the big black across the prairie at a fast pace. Mindful of the sheriff's admonition, he glanced behind him frequently, although he knew he had

135

little to fear from that direction. Anyone who might have noticed him leave town and had an idea of trailing him would just be wasting his time against Shadow's speed and endurance. In fact, he was not at all apprehensive about the trip to the Triangle D. Coming back would be a different matter. However, his customary vigilance was in no wise abated. He noted the movements of birds on the wing, the reactions of little animals in the brush. His gaze was constantly roving over his surroundings.

For a while the trail ran over open prairie. Then it entered a region of scattered brush which thickened now and then to wall the trail with chaparral. Slade's vigilance increased. He reached a spot about halfway to the Triangle D *casa* where he could see ahead for more than a quarter of a mile, after which the brush closed in again and the trail curved through thickets of catclaw and prickly pear with occasional large trees looming high above the general level of the brush. He rounded the curve and jerked Shadow to a halt, hand dropping to a gun butt.

A few yards ahead, shadowed by the foliage of a tall tree that spread its branches across the track, a man lay on his back, his arms wideflung. The front of his faded gray shirt was wet with a dark stain. His eyes were closed and his breast rose and fell quickly and jerkily to labored breathing. At the edge of the trail a horse, split reins trailing, nibbled at the sparse grass. A glance showed Slade that it bore a Triangle D brand. Looked like some skulduggery had cut loose out here on the peaceful range; and the fellow, who wore cowhand garb and was quite likely one of Dawson's riders, looked to be in a bad way.

With a muttered oath, Slade dismounted and strode forward. He had almost reached the prostrate man when a slight rustling in the foliage above caused him to jerk his head up.

But not quite quickly enough. A tight loop whizzed down from among the leaves and dropped over his shoulders. A terrific jerk and he was hurled from his feet to strike the ground with stunning force. At the same instant the "wounded" man leaped erect, gun in hand. The black muzzle, rock steady, yawned at the prostrate Ranger.

"All right, Clay," he called. "I've got him covered. Come on down."

There was a scrambling and scuffling overhead and a second man slid down the tree trunk. He regarded Slade with an evil grin.

"Looks like the great El Halcon ain't so smart as he's set up to be," he jeered. "Falling for a moldy old trick like that."

"Stow the gab," the other said curtly. "Haul him up and get his hardware and take that rope off him. We've got to get away from here before somebody comes along; this is a travelled trail."

The other strode forward, gripped Slade under the arms and hauled him erect. His guns were plucked from their sheaths, the noose that pinned his arms was loosened and flipped over his head. His captor stepped back warily.

"The smart thing would be to plug him and leave him here," he growled.

"Maybe," the other conceded, "but orders are orders and you know what happens to folks who don't follow 'em."

The man Clay muttered an oath but didn't argue the point. "All right, you," he ordered, "fork your bronk, and don't try anything or you *will* stay here."

Although still half dazed by the shock of the fall, Slade had sense enough not to offer resistance. To do so would only get him a slug or a belt over the head with a gun barrel. Opportunity might offer later—maybe. He glanced at his captors. They were big men, both of them, one rather tall, the other, the man Clay, short and squat but with a prodigious breadth of shoulder.

The gun holder kept him covered as he mounted. Clay forked the horse bearing the Triangle D burn and unlimbered a Winchester, swinging the muzzle around in Slade's direction. The other holstered his pistol and led a second horse from the brush; it bore a Mexican brand.

"Turn left past the tree and keep going," he told Slade. "Don't make a try at giving us the slip if you know what's good for you. Clay's long gun carries quite a ways and he's got a itchy trigger finger. Get going!"

Slade obeyed; there was nothing else to do. His head had cleared and he was seething with anger, directed at himself. It *was* an old trick, and he fell for it like a dumb yearling. Yes, an old trick, but with some novel and effective variations. The Indians used to "play dead" to lure unwary travellers into an ambuscade. Later, outlaws employed the same procedure. But a man playing dead can hold his breath just so long, and keen eyes could note the slight movement of his chest when he was forced to exhale. The simulation of the spasmodic breathing of a badly wounded man was disarming, with the stolen Triangle D brand horse to further allay suspicion. Still, blast it! he should have been on the lookout for some real smart expedient. The devil knew he'd had warnings enough and examples of the outfit's diabolical cunning. Not hard to figure how the thing was worked. His acceptance of Dawson's invitation was overheard and the trap set.

Well, he'd made a slip and would very likely pay the ultimate price for it. He had no idea what was in store for him, but one thing was sure for certain, it wouldn't be pleasant.

Pushing through the straggle of growth, his captors close behind, he reached a faint track that wound in a southerly direction with the thorny brush encroaching on either side. There was a decided slope to the ground and soon the way led along the bottom of a ravine. The going was fairly rough but the pair evidently knew the road.

"You break trail, Sid," Clay told his companion. The other slipped past Slade to lead the way and pressed forward at a good pace. Soon a little stream fed by a spring which bubbled from under the left bank, now almost a cliff, paralleled the trail, such as it was. Slade studied his surroundings and saw that an attempt to escape would just be a quick way of committing suicide. He grimly resigned himself to patience; maybe he'd get a break.

Deeper and deeper grew the ravine, walled on either side by bristles of thorny growth. It curved now and then but was mostly a straight trend south. From various indications, Slade judged it had once been the bed of a river long since dried up.

After nearly an hour of riding the growth began to edge away from the trail and Slade fostered a hope that opportunity to make a dash for freedom might present itself. But Sid rode directly in front of him, blocking the way, and Clay brought up the rear with ready rifle.

The growth fell back more and more and they entered a clearing which was a hundred yards or so in width and perhaps thrice that in length. And in the clearing stood a weather-beaten cabin similar to many that dotted the section, former homes of hunters or trappers. Sid led the way to the door.

"Okay," he said to Slade, "unfork and into the shack."

It was only a breath of sound that escaped Slade's lips as he swung down from the saddle, but it was enough for Shadow. Instantly the big horse bolted, tearing across the clearing and crashing into the growth and out of sight. Slade knew he'd stick around and await his call, keeping out of sight until it came. Poor cayuse might have a long wait this time.

Clay swore roundly, but Sid shrugged his shoulders. "Let the hellion go," he said. "This feller won't be needing him anymore and you can't tie onto a horse like that; attract attention and somebody would remember who used to ride him. Inside, feller."

Slade pushed open the door and entered, his captors treading close on his heels. A single glance around showed him that the single big room had known recent occupancy. There were bunks built along the walls, tumbled blankets on them, half a dozen chairs, stacks of staple provisions on shelves, several rifles resting on hooks. There was a solidly built table and rusty iron stove.

"All right," Clay said, "sit down at that table and put your hands flat on top of it."

Slade did so. The table was rather low and he had difficulty getting his knees under the side board to which the top was nailed. He extended his hands, palms down, as he was bid. Clay walked to a shelf, on which he placed the Ranger's long-barrelled guns, shoving them well back so that there would be no danger of them falling off. Slade eyed them longingly. Might as well be in Mexico for any good they were liable to do him.

Sid, who had been standing near the door, his gun ready for instant action, addressed his companion.

"I'm hustling to get the Boss," he said. "He'll be tickled pink to know we've got the hellion and will be hightailing here. I won't be gone long. Hadn't we better tie the feller up?"

Clay shook his head. He fetched a second chair, sat down directly opposite Slade and tilted the chair comfortably against the wall, which was less than five feet from the table.

"This is better," he said, cradling his gun in his lap. "Tie a jigger up and figure he's safe and you're liable to get careless. He wiggles loose when you ain't looking and is on top of you 'fore you know it. This way if he makes a move I'll drill him dead center."

"All right," Sid said, looking dubious, "but if you let him slip through your fingers, what the Boss will do to you won't be nice."

"He won't do any slippin'," Clay replied confidently. "You go ahead and don't bother about me."

Sid grunted and left the cabin, closing the door behind him. A moment later the beat of his horse's hoofs faded away in the distance, evidently backtracking the trail by which they had reached the cabin. Slade studied the cabin and its contents. Very likely, he thought, it was an isolated hangout for the bunch, where they gathered to set out on forays that took them far afield. He had suspected that something of the sort might exist, but had not expected to find it in the manner which he did. His gaze came back to Clay, who sat watching him.

"One thing's sure for certain, you ain't a talking jigger," remarked the outlaw. "Ain't opened your mouth once."

"What was the use?" Slade replied. "I figured talking wouldn't help matters so far as I was concerned. What do you figure to do with me?"

Clay shrugged his shoulders. "That's up to the Boss," he said. "He's sorta riled against you. He ain't the sort of feller that takes kind to somebody else hornin' in on his good thing. Guess he figures he can do without you. He'll tell you when he sees you."

Slade tried a shot in the dark. "He's got a good business in town," he observed carelessly.

"Uh-huh, until you showed up everything was

going along fine," said Clay. Which was certainly not very informative; the shot had missed. He had hoped Clay might make mention of the legitimate business the Boss was in, which would have given Slade a line on him, did he by some miracle get a chance to use it. He studied Clay intently, trying to spot some weakness in the man's make-up, some way to distract his attention long enough to allow him to get his hands under the edge of the table. Could he do so, he'd flip the table into the outlaw's lap and take his chances of being on top of him before he could get his gun into action.

But if Clay had a weakness that might be played upon, he didn't show it. He sat vigilant and alert, his finger crooked around the trigger of the gun that rested in his lap, the muzzle pointing at Slade. Every time Slade would shift a little in his chair to ease his cramped position, the gun muzzle would jut forward a trifle and Clay's thumb would drop onto the milled tip of the hammer; he was taking no chances. Slade realized how a mouse must feel when tortured by a cat, being allowed to move a little in an escape attempt, then being hooked back by a clawed paw.

The minutes dragged past. Slade began calculating how long it would take Sid to reach town and fetch the Boss. Three hours would be a liberal estimate, a little more, a little less. And the first hour was about gone. And Clay sat alert as ever, his vigilance not relaxing for an instant.

Slade's muscles were aching from strain, his nerves tightening with the intolerable suspense. Blast it! anything would be better than this. Better to make a desperate try for the outlaw, even if it got him a bullet, which it very probably would. His arms were beginning to have a wooden feel. The sharp edge of the side board was cutting into his knees. He moved them the merest trifle and felt the table tip up the fraction of an inch. A wild hope surged through his brain. Clay was watching his hands, but he wasn't watching his knees! And his long legs gave him an excellent purchase on the floor with his feet. He relaxed a moment, summoning all his strength for one prodigious effort.

A deep breath, his muscles tensed. He surged erect, putting the last iota of thrust into his legs.

The heavy table flew through the air as if it had taken unto itself wings. Clay's gun boomed. The bullet thudded into the thick wood of the top. Then table, chair and outlaw hit the floor together with a splintering crash. Slade hurtled over the wreckage and closed with Clay. The gun, dashed from Clay's hand, clattered along the floor boards just out of reach. Both men fought madly to gain it.

Over and over they rolled, hitting, kneeing, butting, clutching for the weapon that meant life. Slade's knee struck it and it skittered along a little farther as Clay's hand all but closed on the butt. The outlaw howled a baffled curse followed by a roar of pain as Slade's fist smashed his nose flat. With a mighty effort he whirled the Ranger sideways before his clutching fingers reached their objective.

They landed on top of the chair, which went to pieces beneath them. Clay grabbed a leg and brought it crashing down on Slade's head. As the Ranger sagged under the force of the blow, Clay got the gun. Slade's hand shot out and gripped his wrist. His head was whirling, waves of blackness were coiling about him. With the last remnants of his failing strength he jerked Clay's wrist back and down. His eyes were blinded, his ears deafened by the explosion of the gun right in his face.

Clay screamed, a horrible bubbly scream that rose to a retching shriek. His boot heels beat a weird tattoo on the floor. His body flopped like a beheaded chicken, blood gushing from his bullet-slashed throat. He shuddered from head to foot, and was still.

Slade struggled to his knees, tried to gain his feet, and plunged forward on his face to lie as motionless as the dead man by his side.

FOURTEEN

When Slade recovered consciousness he knew he must have been out for quite a while. The blood was clotted on Clay's throat and the angle of sunlight streaming through a window had changed appreciably. His head ached prodigiously and he felt weak and sick. For a moment he lay still, trying to get his mind to functioning normally. A rush of apprehension flooded his brain. Sid! The Boss! At any minute they might barge in on him! Gasping and retching, he scrambled to his feet and reeled to the shelf on which Clay had placed his guns. He fumbled them down and holstered them. Then with a quick glance at the dead outlaw he staggered to the door and flung it open. Leaning against the jamb, he whistled a shrill note.

There was a crashing in the brush on the far side of the clearing and Shadow bulged into view. With a snort he trotted to the cabin. Slade's strength was returning and he managed to mount without too much difficulty. Settling his feet in the stirrups, he turned the horse's head south. The devil only knew where this crack in the hills lead to, but he didn't dare go back the way he had come and chance meeting Sid and those who would be with him. He was in no shape for another desperate battle; for any kind of a battle, for that matter. There was a slight haze before his eyes and his movements were jerky.

However, the feel of the powerful horse beneath him was revivifying. He straightened in the saddle, the cobwebs clearing from his brain.

"Let's go, feller," he said. Shadow started forward at his smooth running walk.

From the far end of the clearing sounded a shout. Slade twisted around to see half a dozen men surging from the brush. The leader was tall and slender; that was about all Slade could make of him. He saw the flashing gleam of a raised rifle.

"Trail, Shadow, trail!" he called.

Instantly the great horse plunged ahead, his hoofs drumming the ground. A rifle cracked and the bullet whined close. Slade leaned low over Shadow's neck, urging him to greater speed with voice and hand. The big black responded nobly, slugging his head above the bit, snorting, his glorious black mane tossing and rippling in the wind of his passing. With lead storming all around him, he flashed into the cover of the protecting brush.

But the going was hard and Slade could hear the shouts and curses of the pursuers. They, too, were well mounted and they showed no intention of giving up the chase.

A mile fled past, and the better part of another, and still he could hear voices and the drumming of hoofs. Unable to give his best over the broken ground, Shadow was barely holding his own. So far the trail was winding, but should they reach a long straight stretch the outlaws could bring their rifles to bear. Slade loosened his own Winchester in the saddle boot and grimly waited. His head was clear at last, his vision no longer impaired. They might get him in the end, but he'd take a few along with him when he took the Big Jump.

He careened around a sharp bend and the trail straightened out for a hundred yards or so. He sent Shadow scudding to where it again curved, pulled him to a halt and whirled him around. Unlimbering the Winchester, he sat tense and ready, the long gun at full cock.

Around the far bend tore the pursuit. They saw the grim figure sitting with lined rifle and jerked their mounts to a slithering halt. The leader's horse reared high just as Slade pulled trigger and got the slug intended for its rider. Down it went in a floundering heap. A second fell over it and the pursuit was thrown into wild confusion. Slade emptied the magazine as fast as he could pull trigger. Through the torrent of curses knifed a yell of pain, and another. Slade whirled Shadow and sent him racing around the bend. He loaded the Winchester, sheathed it and relaxed.

"Now you're all set, horse," he said. "You've got a head start and nothing more to worry about. June along, feller, we came out of this a lot better than I expected for a while."

But as the rugged track flowed on and on between the steep banks of the ravine, Slade himself began to have something to worry about. The sun set in sullen splendor, the twilight deepened, the stars bloomed in the sky and the walls of brush on either side were ebony blocks of shadow. His head still ached, although not so sharply as before, every muscle was sore, even his bones seemed affected by the terrific battering he had taken in the course of the struggle with Clay, and he was famished. And still the unseen trail flowed on.

However, all things come to him who waits— if he waits long enough—and sometimes to him who doesn't. And that infernal crack in the hills finally did come to an end and Slade found himself riding over level prairie. He knew he must be far south of San Antonio and somewhat to the west. Getting his bearings by the stars, he rode east by north. After an hour or so he reached a well-travelled trail running south by south. This he reasoned must be the San Antonio-Brownsville road. On it he turned north. Somewhere not too far ahead should be the village of Pleasanton, about thirty miles south of San Antonio and once one of the cattle concentration points on the old Western Trail to Dodge City, Kansas. Nearly an hour later he saw lights sprinkling the prairie. Soon he was on the outskirts of the town, then riding its main street, which was a continuation of the trail.

As he passed an exceptionally large tree, one of the many which shaded the street, Slade recalled a grimly amusing story concerning a Pleasanton tree. Seemed that under one of them, trail drivers—drinking and gambling in its shade—caused such a disturbance that a civic-minded saloon owner who had a place nearby built a room for them high in its branches, so that they could woo Bacchus and the goddess of chance without keeping everybody awake.

That was fine until a somewhat inebriated cowboy, while trying to climb to the lofty gaming emporium, fell and busted his neck. After which, despite the protests of sleepy villagers, the "boys" resumed their wooing of the fickle goddess on dependable ground beneath the tree. Slade wondered if it could be the same tree.

Shortly after passing the tree, he spotted what he sought, a livery stable where Shadow could acquire accommodations.

"Fine looking cayuse," observed the stable keeper. "I'll treat him right, and he'll be here when you come for him; I've got a sawed-off that says so. Say, you 'pear to have been in a shindig."

"Took a tumble," Slade replied, with truth.

"Must have been quite a tumble," the keeper remarked dryly and refrained from further comment.

"Something to eat?" he replied to Slade's question. "The Three Horns saloon right around the next corner puts out good chuck, and the drinks are average. Place to sleep? I got a room for rent over the stalls. Nothing fancy, but it's clean, and no bugs. Okay, you can put your rig in it—first door at head of the stairs. There's a trough and soap and towel in back if you'd like to wash."

"Nothing I'd like better," Slade accepted gratefully.

A sluice in the icy water greatly improved his well being, aside from his gnawing hunger. That he would take care of without delay. He had no trouble locating the Three Horns and when he entered nobody paid him any attention and the bartender who poured the drink he felt he needed merely voiced a pleasant greeting. Evidently wandering cowhands were no novelty in the place. After downing the snort he sat at a table and ordered everything in sight.

His hunger assuaged, he felt just about his normal self again. Ordering a final cup of coffee, he leaned back comfortably in his chair, rolled and lighted a cigarette and gave himself over to reflection.

Well, a gentleman with city experience had

evidently introduced to San Antonio some novel methods of acquiring crooked money, but he was willing to wager that the "syndicate" started out as a brush-popping outlaw bunch specializing in widelooping and an occasional stage holdup or bank robbery. Nothing mysterious or outstanding about them, except unusually snake-blooded ruthlessness, and a leader with more than average brain power.

"Blast it! why did that poor devil of a horse have to stand on its hind legs when it did?" he asked the unresponsive coffee cup. "Otherwise I'd have gotten him dead center. Oh, it was him, all right. No doubt in my mind as to that, although I couldn't prove it; never did get a good look at his face. Well, he'll slip, sooner or later; his kind always does."

Which was a comforting thought. His problem was to stay alive until the desirable event occurred. Which, recent happenings taken into consideration, promised to be something of a chore. He pinched out his cigarette and headed for the livery stable and bed.

Mid-morning found him in the saddle, headed north. He forded the Medina River, twelve miles south of San Antonio, and reached the town without further mishap. After stabling his horse, he repaired to the sheriff's office, where he found Rader in something of a dither.

"So you made it!" he exclaimed in relieved

153

tones. "By gosh! this time I figured you were a goner. Dawson was in this morning asking about you. Said you never did show up at his place. Him and his boys are combing the brush for you. Said they'd be back later. What happened?"

Slade told him. The sheriff swore till the air was blue.

"What the devil are we going to do?" he concluded helplessly.

"Await opportunity, and act when it comes," Slade replied.

"Sounds fine!" the sheriff snorted. "But opportunity always 'pears to be a couple of jumps ahead of us."

"We'll catch up," Slade predicted cheerfully.

"Anyhow you're thinnin' 'em out," said Rader. "I done lost count how many altogether."

"Yes," Slade agreed, "but the brains of the outfit is still going strong, unless I'm mistaken. That is if he didn't bust his ornery neck when his horse went down with him, which, unfortunately I doubt."

"And you think you know who he is?"

"Yes, but I can't prove it, and until I can, conjecture is futile."

"At least you know who to look for, and that's something," observed the sheriff.

"Yes," Slade repeated, "I know who to keep an eye on, but keeping an eye on a snake isn't

154

enough; you have to draw its fangs if you want to live securely."

"You'll draw 'em, on that I'm willing to bet a hatful of pesos," Rader declared.

"Anyhow, your confidence is inspiring," Slade smiled. "Well, here's hoping. Let's go get something to eat."

As the day drew to a close, Slade played a hunch that Yolanda would be at La Culebra and bent his steps in that direction.

She was. At a table with Serge Kendricks. Followed a few minutes of general conversation, during which Slade made light of his bruised face and skinned knuckles. Both looked anxious but did not press for an explanation. A little later, Kendricks left to attend to some chores.

"How were things at the Calaorra last night?" Slade asked casually.

"Very good," Yolanda replied. "Plenty of busi-ness and everything went smoothly, except Mr. Allen appeared to be in a very bad temper about something. He snapped at everybody, and found fault."

"He was there then?" Slade asked needlessly; she'd just said that he was.

"Yes, he was there," she replied. "I went in early and he was there when I got there."

Slade nodded. Another lead had petered out.

Just the same he did not in the least alter his

opinion based on a careful analysis of all he had observed and been able to learn about that slippery gentleman, that Norman Allen was the brains of the syndicate. He'd hoped that Allen might have been injured when his horse fell, or perhaps nicked by one of the bullets he poured into the bunch and in consequence would not have been able to make it back to town the day before. Which would have provided another link in the chain, an important one. Being uninjured, however, he would have had plenty of time to do so, which evidently was the case.

Slade was not yet ready to take the sheriff or anybody else into his confidence. He believed that Allen had no notion that he was suspect, and a slip of the tongue on somebody's part might well put him on his guard, and he was problem enough as it was. Also there was always the chance that he might learn that he, Slade, was a Texas Ranger, which would further complicate matters.

So long as he believed he had only El Halcon, another smart owlhoot with designs on his preserves, to deal with, Slade believed he'd be ready to match wits with the interloper and fight the thing out to a finish. But let him learn that he was suspect by a Texas Ranger on his trail and he might well slip out of sight and head for parts unknown; and running him down would be a chore, even if there was evidence against him which would justify running him down, which there wasn't.

Furthermore, a good undercover man never sought help unless it was definitely to his advantage to do so; a necessity, in fact. So he'd keep his own counsel for a while longer and continue to play a lone hand.

Having reached a decision to that effect, he said "so long" to Yolanda and left La Culebra in a cheerful frame of mind.

FIFTEEN

Will Dawson and his thorn-tattered cowboys rode into town shortly after dark and trooped into the sheriff's office.

"So here you are!" he rumbled in an accusing voice that was belied by the glad light in his eyes. "Where the devil you been? Might have known you'd come outa it okay. Look at me! Lost half my shirt. Will take a week to pick the brambles outa my hide. The next time you get lost you can stay lost. Why can't you be dependable like Rader here? Always know where to find *him*—warmin' the seat of his pants on that chair. Put her there, son, it's good to see you safe and sound, which was more than I hoped for after I learned you were among the missing."

He grinned and shook hands warmly. "Come on, everybody," he said. "This calls for a mite of celebrating, and I'm hungry as all blazes, too. Come along, Slade, you can tell me what happened after I've had a couple of snorts and see a full plate in front of me. Let's go!"

While Dawson ate hugely, Slade regaled him with an account of his misadventure of the day before. The rancher listened intently, mumbling oaths through mouthfuls of steak and potatoes.

"The blasted wind spiders!" he growled when Slade paused. "I've a notion to form a vigilance committee and clean out the whole nest of snakes."

"Got to find the nest first," the sheriff interpolated.

"We'll find it, sooner or later," declared Dawson. "Never saw one that could keep hid forever. And when we do!"

Dawson had finished eating and was ordering drinks when a man, his clothes dusty from hard riding, entered and glanced about as if in search of someone. He spoke to the bartender who gestured toward the table occupied by Slade and his companions. The man turned and hurried across the room.

"Sheriff," he said when he reached the table, "the Pleasanton bank was robbed this afternoon of nearly fifty-thousand dollars and the hellions headed this way into your county. We figured you should know about it so you could keep an eye open for them."

"The devil you say!" exclaimed Rader. "Anybody get a look at 'em?"

"They were masked," the informant replied. "But last night a big feller who sure had the look of an owlhoot rode into town after dark. Stayed all night and sort of looked things over in the morning before he rode off again. Reckon he was there to get the lowdown on thebank."

"Could be," the sheriff conceded gravely, twinkling his eyes at Slade. "Was anybody hurt?"

"Cashier shot through the shoulder, a clerk got

a busted arm," the man replied. "Cashier may not make it, pretty bad hurt."

The sheriff's face turned stern. "All right," he said, "I'll be on the lookout for them."

"And what do you know about that!" he exclaimed when the man from Pleasanton headed to the bar for a drink. "So they're really branching out."

"Merely going back to their original activities, now that things have been getting a mite hot in town," Slade said. "That's the way they started out. I expect once they're rounded up we'll find they have operated in a number of sections before coming here."

Suddenly he leaned forward, his eyes glowing. "Sheriff," he said, "let's play a hunch."

"A hunch?"

"Yes, a hunch that the devils headed for that cabin in which I was held prisoner, to hole up till the loot is divided, then to slip into town one by one so as not to attract attention."

"But do you think they'd do it after you escaping from there?" the sheriff objected.

"Why not?" Slade countered. "They'd have no reason to believe I'd be coming back right away, and nobody else knows about the shack or just where it is. I've got a hunch they'll do just that."

"Okay, we'll play it," said Rader. "You coming along, Will?"

160

"You're darned right I am," growled Dawson. "I got something coming to me after that sashay through the brush. That goes for my boys, too. Let's go!"

"Wait," Slade counselled. "Take it easy for a while; no telling who may be keeping an eye on us, and the devils are smart. If we go busting out of here all together, somebody may catch on and circle around by way of some short cut only they know and tip off the cabin. Mr. Dawson will stick around for half an hour, then call his boys and 'head for home'. They'll wait for us out where the trail enters the thick brush. You and I, Rader, will remain here another half hour. Outside, you return to your office and I'll head for my hotel. We'll meet at the livery stable where I keep my horse and ride out of town from there. Okay?"

"Sounds smart to me," said Dawson. "Son, you got plenty of savvy. You figure you can locate that shack in the dark?"

"Yes, I can locate it," Slade answered. "I'll know where to turn off and once in that gulley there's no missing it." Dawson nodded, and ordered another drink.

"Here comes Norm," he remarked, "grinning as usual."

As Allen approached, Slade's keen glance noted that he did not walk as smoothly as usual; he appeared to limp a little. He was smiling his customary genial smile, but it seemed to Slade that he sensed a tinge of mockery in that smile as Allen's pale eyes rested on his face.

Allen chatted pleasantly for a couple of minutes, ordered a drink sent over and sauntered back to the bar where he mingled with the drinkers. Watching him closely, Slade was sure as to the limp. He also noted that one of the men with whom Allen spoke turned slightly and glanced in his direction. It appeared that he was under discussion and the glance was an instinctive reaction toward the subject of conversation. Could mean nothing at all, then again it might mean plenty. He marked the fellow for possible future reference.

When he looked that way again, the man was nowhere in sight.

"Norm's okay," observed Dawson. "Always does the right thing. No wonder he's making a go of it here." He lowered his voice. "I'm not supposed to mention such things, but being a bank director I happen to know he's stashin' away plenty. This place is paying off big, bigger'n you'd think."

"I don't doubt it," Slade remarked with a dryness that was lost on Dawson.

Leaning back comfortably in their chairs and smoking, the three indulged in what appeared to possible observers to be casual conversation, but which really was careful going over of details of the contemplated raid.

Finally Dawson glanced at his watch and stood

up. Bidding a loud good night to Slade and the sheriff he approached the bar, where his hands had gathered after they finished eating.

"Okay, boys," he called. "Down your slugs and come along; we've got work to do tomorrow. So long, Norm, see you in church."

The Triangle D bunch trooped out. Slade and the sheriff sat on at the table, talking and smoking. After a while Rader remarked,

"Isn't it about time we were moving?"

Slade glanced at the clock behind the bar. "Yes," he replied. "If we can't leave now without arousing suspicion we never can."

"And you figure somebody may be keeping tabs on us?" the sheriff asked as they stood up.

"Somebody is," Slade replied definitely. "Let's go."

Outside the saloon, after a word or two, they parted company, Slade heading in one direction, Rader in another.

Slade walked slowly, watching the reflections in the windows across the street, and saw nothing to indicate he was followed. When he reached the hotel, he lounged for several minutes in its shadow, then made his way to the stable by a circuitous route, confident he was not tailed. He found the sheriff mounted and waiting for him. It took but a few minutes to get the rig on Shadow and lead him from the stable. With a final glance around, they headed west at a fast pace and did not draw rein until they saw the dark clump of the waiting Triangle D outfit loom at the edge of the thicker growth.

With the plainsman's unerring instinct for distance and direction, Slade led the way to the great tree which marked the spot where the hidden track joined the main trail. Pushing their way through the straggle of thorny growth they reached it.

"More brambles!" groaned Dawson. "There goes the rest of my shirt! Son, you can pick the darndest places to get into."

"Not so bad from here on," Slade consoled him. "Don't know what we'll find at the end of it, though."

"More brambles with longer thorns, the chances are," Dawson grunted. "Let's go!"

Slade carefully estimated the distance covered as they paced along. It was a night of clear moonlight and the rough trail posed no great difficulties. Finally he called a halt.

"We travel by shank's mare from here on," he announced, dismounting. "Leave the bronks with one man to keep an eye on them. If we go clattering along over the rocks on horseback, we'll let everybody this side of Mexico know we're coming."

"And if the sidewinders are there, we'll get a reception we won't like," added Rader. "For Pete's sake, everybody be quiet!"

Silently they stole along, until they reached the point where the track entered the clearing, which the moonlight rendered almost as bright as day. The two north windows of the cabin glowed golden.

"They're in there!" the sheriff whispered exultantly.

"Yes, they're in there," Slade agreed. "Also, there's a moon in the sky."

"What do you mean by that?" asked Dawson.

"I mean," Slade replied, "that all of a sudden I don't like this set-up. Look over there at that clump of horses tethered in plain view in front of the shack. I recall there's a lean-to with feed boxes for horses just beyond the cabin. Why aren't they sheltered under the lean-to instead of being right out in the open where they can't even graze? Looks like they were deliberately left there to announce to anybody that their riders are inside. No, I don't like it. Wait a minute, now."

He surveyed the cabin, his black brows drawing together, a sign that El Halcon was doing some hard thinking.

"Seems to me that I recall a window in the back of the cabin," he said at length. "I've a notion I can slip through the brush and reach the back wall of the shack without being spotted; I'm going to try it. I want to look into the cabin before we go sashaying across that clearing."

"You'll be taking a chance," muttered the sheriff.

"Less than we'll all be taking if we venture

into the open without knowing what we're up against," Slade countered. "Keep a close watch on the cabin and if the hellions come out and start to mount, let them have it."

Silently he glided into the brush and vanished from their sight.

"Moves like an Indian," breathed Dawson. "Not a sound out of him. I reckon he'll be okay."

Slowly and carefully, Slade wormed his way through the thorny brush. Here at the edge of the clearing it was not so closely grown as elsewhere and posed no insurmountable difficulty.

Completing the half circle around the clearing, he peered out and saw the rear of the cabin only a few yards distant. There was a window in the back wall, glowing with light. He studied it for long minutes and decided nobody was watching the rear. Crossing the patch of moonlight was a ticklish business and he breathed a sigh of relief when he reached the wall. Hugging close against the chinked logs, he edged along until he could peer inside.

His fears had not been groundless. Standing at each north window, a rifle leaning against the wall by his side, was a man who gazed intently toward the dark mouth of the trail. Five other men lounged about the room, weapons ready to hand. Slade paused a moment, then glided back into the brush. He noted that there was also a back door which stood just a crack ajar.

The posse jumped with low exclamations when he reappeared from the growth as silently as a ghost.

"Don't do that again, son," muttered Dawson. "You scared me half out of my skin."

"If we'd started across that clearing you'd likely have been scared all the way out," Slade replied. "Yes, they're in there, all set to mow us down when we moved into the moonlight. As it is, we'll take them from the rear and *they'll* be the ones to get the surprise. In through the back door and get the drop on them. We'll have to work fast, and I've a notion they won't give up without a fight; they're desperate characters. All set to go? Come along, then, and don't make a noise."

The crawl through the brush was negotiated without mishap. The posse paused in the straggle to the rear of the cabin. Slade motioned for silence, listened intently for a moment. From inside the cabin came a low hum of voices, no sounds of excitement or alarm.

"All right," he whispered. "Fast, now."

In a flying wedge, Slade at the point, Rader and Dawson close behind, they hit the door, flung it wide open and poured into the room. The stunned outlaws stood with gaping mouths. Sheriff Rader's voice rang out—

"Elevate! You are under—"

That was as far as the sheriff got before the ball opened with a roar of gunfire.

SIXTEEN

It was a wild and savage battle in the confines of the single room. Men strove breast to breast, guns blazing, striking with the barrels, wrestling, grappling. The outlaws, knowing no mercy would be shown, fought like cornered rats, as vicious and as deadly, ready to die if they could just take somebody with them.

They died, riddled with bullets, shooting as long as they had strength to pull trigger. Within seconds the floor was littered with bodies. Four of the cowboys were down, two badly wounded. Blood visored Dawson's face with scarlet. The sheriff's left arm flapped helplessly, numbed by a slug that tore a shallow furrow through the biceps. Slade was bleeding from a nicked shoulder and a creased hand. He lowered his smoking guns and peered through the fog at the shambles. Walking to the front door he threw it open to clear the air.

"Here's one that ain't dead yet," called Dawson, mopping at his bullet-gashed cheek with a ragged sleeve.

Slade walked to where the dying man lay and bent over him. Glazing eyes glared up into his.

"Feller," he said, "you're going to take the Big Jump. Why not come clean before you go? Tell us who's the head of your outfit."

The man continued to glare. His mouth worked jerkily. Halting words frothed over his blood-bubbling lips, "G-go—go—go—get—shot!" His eyes closed and he lapsed into unconsciousness. Three minutes later he was dead.

"Anyhow you have to give the horned toad credit for guts," Dawson observed with grudging admiration.

"A hard man to the last," Slade agreed. "Well, it looks like we cleaned up here, even though we didn't learn anything. Nose around and I expect you'll find the loot from the Pleasanton bank. How are the boys?"

"Whetsal and Kearns got it pretty bad," Rader replied. "They need a doctor."

Slade beckoned two of the younger cowhands. "Hightail to where we left the horses and have them brought here," he directed. "I have bandage and salve in my saddle pouches; I'll do what I can. You two fork your bronks and head back to the main trail. One of you stay there to show the way into the gulley while the other makes it to town as fast as he can to find a doctor and bring him here. Get going!"

The pair sped from the cabin. Slade examined the wounded. He had a smashed shoulder, another a slug through the chest, high up. The other two had suffered leg wounds that Slade did not consider serious aside from the bleeding, which he stanched as best he could with the makeshift materials at hand. Nor was Rader much hurt.

"I think we can risk moving Whetsal and Kearns onto the bunks where they'll be more comfortable," he told Dawson. "Give me a hand. I'll see what I can do as soon as the horses get here."

Horses! He was struck by a sudden idea. "Be back in a minute," he told the rancher and left the cabin.

Talking soothingly to the outlaws' tethered horses, he approached them and gave them a careful once-over, especially one that stood with hanging head, front feet widespread. He quickly got the rig off the animal and rubbed it down a bit with his hands.

"That'll hold you for a while, feller," he told the cayuse. "I think you'll make it okay."

With a final pat on the reeking neck, he returned to the cabin.

"Just as I expected," he told Rader and Dawson. "A horse out there wringing wet with sweat and very nearly done in. The hellion who left town ahead of us almost killed him getting here to tip off the bunch that we'd be on our way. If we'd tried to cross that clearing we'd have never known what hit us."

His hearers stared at him and sweat mingled with the blood on Dawson's face as he mopped it with his other sleeve.

"But how in blazes did the sidewinder catch on?" he wanted to know. "We didn't tell anybody we were coming here."

"No, but a smart devil figured out just what we would be likely to do and took precautions against it," Slade returned, " 'Pears he's always a jump ahead of us."

"Uh-huh, a jump ahead, but this time he didn't jump far enough," put in the sheriff, glancing significantly at the bodies on the floor. "Takes a long jump to get the jump on—El Halcon."

"Yes, we owe it to you, son, for being alive right now," added the rancher. "Here come the horses."

With ointment and bandages, Slade went to work on the seriously wounded. After a while he stepped back wearing a satisfied expression.

"I've a notion that'll hold them till the doctor gets here," he said. "They both got it pretty hard, but they're tough and seeing as they haven't bled to death, I figure they'll make the grade. Did you find the loot?"

"Every dollar of it, still in sacks," the sheriff replied. "Those hellions were packing considerable in their pockets but nothing else that 'peared to be of any value. Want to look it over?"

Slade did, but he didn't learn anything of value from the miscellany of articles of the sort usually carried by range riders. Nor was there anything about their arms or clothing worthy of notice.

"Horses have Mexican burns, except a couple with west Texas brands, which doesn't mean much," he said. "Horses can be bought or traded or stolen and found a long ways from where they got the iron set to their hides."

Turning from the heap of trinkets, he gave the bodies of the slain outlaws a careful once-over. The features of one, badly mangled by a slug that passed through both cheeks, had a vaguely familiar look. He was not positive, but he believed they belonged to the man whose glance he intercepted in the Calaorra, the man who was talking to Norman Allen and who evidently left the saloon shortly afterward.

When the doctor arrived, a couple of hours later, he confirmed Slade's diagnosis of the wounded and commended his ministrations.

"I've a feeling the world lost a fine surgeon when you turned to ranching," he said. "You've got the hands and the eyes, and no nerves. Yes, I think medicine would have been right in your line."

"And anything else he takes a notion to set his hand to," said Dawson. "He'd make a bang-up peace officer."

Sheriff Rader grinned under his mustache and was silent.

"How about moving those punctured jiggers?" asked Dawson.

"Not tonight," the doctor replied decidedly. "Tomorrow we'll see. I'll stay here of course until I'm satisfied they are okay."

"And some of the boys will stay with you," said Dawson. "Now what do you say we get a fire going in the stove and cook something? Plenty of good stuff on those shelves. This sort of thing always makes me hungry and I figure we'll do better on full bellies."

Nobody objected to that and soon an appetizing meal was on the table. The doctor supervised what was given the wounded and pronounced their desire for food a good sign.

Dawn was streaking the sky when they set out for town, the bodies of the outlaws draped across their horses' saddles. The recovered bank money was safely stored in saddle pouches.

"I'll send the bank at Pleasanton a wire," said Rader. "Wouldn't be surprised if they'll be wanting to hand out a reward."

"Should go to Slade, if they do," declared Dawson.

El Halcon smilingly shook his head. "Got a few pesos salted away for a rainy day," he said. "Divide it up among your boys; they earned it, especially those who stopped lead. They did a fine chore and if there's any reward money, let them have a real bust with it."

"They'll have one, all right," chuckled the rancher, "but if things keep on like they've been going, the spread is headed for rack and ruin. Ain't never no work done anymore."

"I've a notion you'll be able to keep on eating," the sheriff commented dryly. "That is if you don't go busted playing poker with those sharks."

"I never lose, except when I don't win," Dawson protested.

There was excitement aplenty in San Antonio that morning. Several citizens who viewed the bodies were of the opinion that they had seen one or more in town, but were vague as to who they might have associated with. Only Norman Allen provided some definite information.

"That one with the hole through both cheeks was in the Calaorra quite a few times recently," he said. "In fact, he was there last night. I spoke to him now and then, as I do with all my customers. Seemed pleasant enough. Always had money although he didn't seem to work. I asked him once who he rode for and he said he rode for the King ranch last but was taking it easy for a few days."

"Biggest outfit in Texas," interpolated the sheriff. "They have plenty of rider turn-over."

"Guess that's so," agreed Allen. "Very likely he did work for them at one time or another." With a smile and a nod he left the office.

"Smart!" Slade muttered to himself. "Covered up beautifully."

A Calaorra bartender corroborated Allen's testimony. "Yes, I remember him, too," he said. " 'Peared to be an all right jigger. 'Tended to his own business but was always ready to talk with anybody who spoke to him first. Yep, he seemed to be okay, but you never can tell."

"Folks are beginning to talk a mite freer," Sheriff Rader commented to Slade. "Not that they've helped us much so far. Anyhow, we must have just about cleaned the nest, don't you think?"

"We've been thinning them out, but it's a big outfit and well organized," Slade replied. "Also, as I said before, the head is still running around loose and until he is taken care of, one way or another, the chore isn't finished. He'll just get another bunch together and keep on operating. Plenty to draw from in this section. That's always the way. Remember the Brocius gang in Arizona, one of the most powerful of its kind the Southwest ever knew. Any number of Curly Bill's men were killed, but not until he was eliminated did the gang cease to function. The same applied to the King Fisher and Sam Bass outfits here in Texas. Only after the death of the leaders did they break up and were no longer a menace. We've got to get the head."

"You'll get him," declared the sheriff. "I have every confidence in you."

"Hope it's not misplaced," Slade smiled. "Well, I'm going to bed. I feel like I'd been drug through a cactus patch and hung on a barbed wire to dry. You'd better get some sleep, too."

"I'm going to," answered the sheriff. "May join Dawson in a drink first. Hope there isn't a poker game going, or he'll forget all about sleep. He's the limit! See you sometime this evening."

Slade repaired to his room and was asleep almost before his head hit the pillow.

SEVENTEEN

When Slade awoke, the red light of the sunset was streaming its level rays through the window. He glowered at it disgustedly.

"Yes, I'm turning into a blasted owl," he growled. "Don't start to hoot till the sun goes down."

He arose in a disgruntled mood, still a bit stiff and sore from his rough and tumble battle with Clay in the cabin. After a bath and a shave he felt better and sallied forth in search of some breakfast. Not wishing to face the habitual hullabaloo of the Calaorra at the moment, he ate in a small and quiet restaurant. After which he relaxed with a cigarette and gave himself over to serious thought.

He debated taking Sheriff Rader fully into his confidence, but decided against it for the time being. The old peace officer was a forthright individual and not good at controlling his facial expressions. Allen, keen eyed and undoubtedly sensitive to impressions, might note a change in his attitude, and Slade believed that the saloonkeeper did not as yet consider himself under suspicion, especially by the officers of the law. Best to keep him that way as long as possible. Believing himself to be immune from official espionage, he was much more likely to make a slip of some kind, although he was definitely not the sort given to making slips.

"You did make one last night, though, when you slid that hellion out to warn your bunch," he apostrophized the saloonkeeper. "That was all I needed to clinch the case against you, in my own mind."

However, he was forced to admit, personal opinions don't carry much weight in a courtroom unless backed by something concrete, and as yet he hadn't a thing on Allen that would stand up in court. Well, maybe he'd get a break. Breaks of a sort had been coming his way of late. Otherwise he wouldn't still be up and kicking. Which was something, all things taken into account. He ordered another cup of coffee and rolled another cigarette.

His mood changed to one of complacency, almost exhilaration. It was good to be alive, good to be confronted by an intriguing battle of wits that would very likely culminate in explosive violence. That was one of the things which sustained his unflagging interest in the Rangers. Always a new problem to face, and solve. Little chance of getting bored in the Rangers. Always like riding toward distant hills that blocked off what was beyond, that quickened curiosity and expectation.

The twilight deepened. The hum of San Antonio's busy night life grew louder. Hoofs clattered as a troop of cowhands rode into town. Outside sounded talk and laughter. Slade chuckled; the owls were beginning to hoot. He pinched out his cigarette and left the restaurant.

Commerce Street was crowded, gay and animated. Slade felt his pulses quicken as he strolled along; perhaps being an owl wasn't so bad after all. There was plenty to interest him, most of all the faces he passed as the throng swirled and eddied, especially at the Fatal Corner where Commerce and Soledad crossed. Here gamblers, barkeeps and dance floor girls paused to pass the time of day before taking up their chores in the various places of entertainment. Plenty of trouble other than the killing of King Fisher and Ben Thompson had started on the Fatal Corner and very likely would again.

Slade chuckled again as he recalled having once read an article dealing with the Fatal Corner killings, which had gravely stated that six *major* homicides had occurred there. Evidently the minor cashing-ins of small fry were not worthy of mention; only such illustrious citizens as King Fisher and Thompson achieved that dubious honor. He wondered what was the Fatal Corner's real tally. A revised version would certainly include the name of Jack Richardson who, according to Sheriff Rader, got his come-uppance in the immediate vicinity by the hand of Norman Allen.

For quite a while he sauntered around, enjoying

178

the cool of the evening and the ceaseless activity of San Antonio's main business section. Inevitably, however, the Calaorra drew him like a lode-stone and he bent his steps in that direction.

The place was already hilarious and there was every promise of a big night. Norman Allen stood at the far end of the bar, near the till, his keen pale eyes constantly roving over the assembly. Slade felt there was nothing that he missed. He returned the saloonkeeper's wave of greeting, found a place at the bar and ordered a drink. Curious but respectful glances were shot in his direction and heads drew together.

"El Halcon," he heard a louder voice say. "They 'low he's an owlhoot, but I'll be hanged if he's been acting like one since he squatted here. He's done more in a week to clean out this section than the sheriff and all the rest of our so-called law officers have done in months."

"Heard they figure to make him a deputy sheriff," said another voice.

"Well, they oughta," said the first speaker. "Then maybe decent folks could live in peace. He's got the right idea—don't fool with 'em, mow 'em down. That's the way the Texas Rangers operate and when a Ranger shows up the snakes go for cover. That's what he really should be—a Ranger. Wonder old McNelty don't sign him up."

"Guess he's sort of a lone wolf and don't like to be tied down. He sure roams around a lot, from what I've heard. Pedro, the orchestra leader, said he knew him over around El Paso way, and another feller was sure he saw him once up in the Panhandle. Yep, he gets around."

"Hope he takes a notion to tie hard and fast here for a spell," remarked the first speaker.

"You can say that double," replied his companion. "We need him."

Slade bit back a grin as the pair glanced in his direction and instinctively lowered their voices. However, he was not at all displeased by their comments. He resumed his study of Norman Allen who appeared to have recovered from whatever had caused him to limp slightly. Once again he moved with easy grace and assurance. He reminded Slade of a great cat stalking its prey, every gesture in perfect harmony—steel claws sheathed in velvet. And a cold, clear brain that missed nothing and functioned with a minimum of error. Very shortly he was to get a revealing glimpse of Norman Allen in action.

He began watching a noisy poker game at a corner table across the room. There were seven players, four cowhands and three Mexicans, and for some reason tempers were getting ruffled, as remarks tossed back and forth among the players indicated. Slade could see that Allen was also keeping an eye on what was going on there. Once he started in that direction, but something deterred him and he turned back to the bar.

Without overture, the row started, and there was nothing phony about it; it was for keeps. The players leaped to their feet as one man, chairs went over, and the table. In an instant there was a whirling tangle of fists and feet with bellowed curses providing a fitting accompaniment to the thud of blows.

Allen bounded across the room before the floor men could get into action. His fist lashed out and the sound of it landing on a jaw was like the crack of a pistol. The recipient went down as if a slug had tapped him. Allen was hitting with both hands and each blow sent an antagonist off his feet.

A man flung an arm around his neck from behind, seeking to throttle him. Allen surged forward and the attacker flew over his shoulder to hit the floor with a crash that set the hanging lamps to dancing; he stayed there.

Off the floor scrambled a big cowhand, mumbling curses through a hedge of splintered teeth, hand reaching for his gun.

Allen leaped back and stood perfectly motionless, two fingers of his left hand gripping the left lapel of his coat, his right spread claw-like against his breast, his eyes fixed on the cowhand. Perfectly motionless, like a rattlesnake poised to strike, as swift and as deadly.

The cowboy saw the death glaring at him from the pale eyes that were like splinters of sapphire and evidently decided that the loss of a few teeth was better than taking the Big Jump; his hand dropped away from his gun and he began mopping his bloody mouth with his neckerchief. His companions, all the fight taken out of them, stood in awkward positions, their hands still.

Allen spoke for the first time. "All right," he said in his quiet, silvery voice. "All right, straighten things up and let's not have any more nonsense. I won't stand for it in my establishment."

As the battered battlers began righting chairs, he turned his back on them and walked to the bar, where he lighted a cigar with a hand that was rock-steady and resumed as if nothing had happened a conversation he had been holding with a man there. Slade regarded him thoughtfully.

"Spring steel and rawhide wrapped up in chain lightning," he murmured. "Quite a gent!"

A little later Sheriff Rader entered and joined Slade at the bar.

"Everything quiet," he announced "See Dawson?"

"Not so far," Slade replied. "Guess he's still sleeping."

"Wouldn't be surprised," nodded Rader. "Was playing poker when I went to bed. Expect he kept it up so long as he could hold his eyes open. They'll hold another fool inquest tomorrow. The county's going busted paying funeral expenses."

Norman Allen moved over to wish them a good evening. "No, I haven't seen Dawson," he answered a question by Rader. "He wasn't here when I came to work. Chances are he'll be around shortly."

The sheriff nodded. "The Pleasanton bank wired they're sending a check for a thousand dollars as a little token of appreciation," he remarked. "A messenger will pick up their money tomorrow."

"Where is it?" Slade asked idly.

"In my office safe, with a deputy standing guard over it," the sheriff replied, lowering his voice.

"Should be safe enough there," Slade commented.

"It is," answered Rader. "Klingman, the deputy, is a dead shot and the kind that keeps his eyes open. Don't figure anybody would try to bust into the courthouse, but I'm taking no chances in this blasted pueblo. The gold fillings in a feller's teeth ain't safe anymore."

Allen chuckled, and ordered a drink on the house. "Got to catch up with some work on my accounts," he said. "Be seeing you later."

A moment later he passed into the back room at the end of the bar, several books under his arm, and closed the door behind him.

Sheriff Rader glanced around. "I see a empty table over by the dance floor and I haven't had anything to eat since I got up," he said. "Have you et?"

Slade nodded. "But I'll have coffee with you," he said. "Don't care for anything more to drink right now."

While the sheriff was putting away a surroundin', the orchestra and the girls arrived. Yolanda waved to Slade, who waved back. He did not approach her, however; he was not in the mood for dancing at the moment.

Dawson and several of his hands rolled in a little later. The rancher, looking a mite bleary-eyed but chipper as usual, joined Slade and Rader at the table.

"I'll have coffee," he said. "Don't feel like anything to eat just yet. Feller told me there was a row in here a little while ago."

"Just a scuffle," Slade replied. "Allen took care of it by himself. They're over at that far table playing poker."

Dawson glanced across the room. "Hmmm!" he said. "From appearances I'd say they were quite 'scuffled'. Look at the jaw on that big one, and the mouth on the jigger across from him. Guess they figured they'd tangled with a buzz saw."

"Norm's sorta salty when he gets started," observed the sheriff. "Remember what I told you about Jack Richardson? If it was Richardson, *he* was a feller who set up to be sorta salty himself."

Dawson glanced toward where Allen was standing at the end of the bar. "Yep, he is," he nodded. "Wouldn't think it to look at him. Ain't very big."

"A stick of dynamite ain't over big, either, but it packs a wallop," Rader observed dryly.

EIGHTEEN

Slade began to grow restless, and a little weary of the unceasing din. He listened to Rader telling Dawson of the reward money the bank was sending and it called to mind the fact that the bank's nearly fifty-thousand dollars was in the sheriff's office with Deputy Caleb Klingman keeping an eye on it. Slade had met Klingman and liked him. Might be a good notion to drop in and share his lonely vigil for a while. Maybe the deputy would like to slip out for coffee or something.

"I'm going to stroll around for a bit," he told his companions. "Be back later, if you aim to stick around."

"Okay," said the sheriff, "but watch your step; somebody may have an eye out for you. Yes, we'll be here for a while. Will's already eyeing that game over there and I feel like taking it easy."

Slade got up and sauntered out. He turned into North Main Avenue from Commerce Street and walked west past Main Plaza until he reached the Courthouse. Mounting the steps, he strolled along the corridor which led to the sheriff's office. He had almost reached it when a strange sound smote his ears, a grinding, creaking sound as if a huge rat were gnawing on metal; it seemed

185

to come from inside the sheriff's office, the door of which stood ajar a crack through which seeped a thread of light.

"Now what the blazes is that jigger doing?" he wondered. At that instant he struck his foot against a big brass spittoon that somebody had carelessly moved away from the wall. Over it went and rolled along the corridor with a prodigious clatter. From inside the office came an exclamation of alarm and a scuffling sound. He stepped forward quickly to reassure Klingman and shoved the door open.

Inside the office a masked man stood beside the sheriff's safe, a drill in one hand, a gun in the other. A second man, also masked, held a low-turned lamp.

Slade hurled himself along the wall as the gun blazed; the bullet ripped through his sleeve. The lamp crashed on the floor and darkness swooped down. Slade jerked his guns and sprayed the office with bullets. A door slammed, footsteps pattered along the corridor into which it opened. Slade bounded forward, tripped over something soft and yielding and sprawled on the floor. Muttering curses, he scrambled to his feet, groped his way to the door and flung it open. He heard a second door slam at the far end of the long corridor and raced toward the sound. But by the time he reached the door and opened it, the dimly lit street beyond was empty.

Holstering his guns he hurried back to the office, filled with apprehension for Klingman. What he had stumbled over was very likely the deputy's body. Reaching the office he fumbled a match from his pocket and struck it. The feeble flicker showed the deputy sprawled on the floor close to the window, his head resting in a pool of blood. The shattered lamp lay beside the safe, in the iron door of which, close to the combination knob, was a steel bit. The brace lay on the floor where the safe-cracker dropped it.

Slade knew where the coroner's office was located, close by. He groped his way to the door and found it unlocked. Striking another match he located a bracket lamp. He touched the match to the wick, removed the lamp from the bracket and returned to the sheriff's office. Placing the lamp on a table he knelt beside Klingman. The deputy was unconscious, breathing stertorously. There was a deep cut in the top of his head. Glancing around, Slade saw that beneath the window was an overturned chair. Evidently Klingman had been sitting close to the open window with his back toward it. Somebody reached in and belted him with a gun barrel or something.

Outside sounded questioning shouts. Somebody had been alarmed by the gunfire and was coming to see what was the matter. Slade walked to the outer door and saw several men hurrying toward the building.

"Hold it," he called. "Somebody hustle over to the Calaorra and fetch Sheriff Rader. Somebody else go get a doctor. Hustle!"

"Okay, feller," a voice shouted. Two men darted away in different directions. Several others followed Slade to the office, halting at the door and peering in curiously.

"Feller, what in blazes happened?" one asked.

Slade gestured to the safe. "What does it look like to you?" he countered.

The speaker peered close. "Looks to me like somebody was trying to drill out the knob and open the safe," he replied.

"Good eyes," Slade commented.

"Did you get any of 'em?"

Slade shook his head. "Don't think so," he replied. "Anyhow, they kept going. I fell over Cale's body and they made it to an outer back door. When I got there nobody was in sight."

"Is Cale bad hurt?"

Slade again knelt beside the deputy, felt his pulse, listened to his breathing.

"I doubt it," he said. "Too much blood for a bad fracture. The chances are he'll have nothing worse than a headache when he gets his senses back. Don't touch anything; I want the sheriff to see the layout just as it is."

He stood up, rolled a cigarette and leaned against the wall, smoking and studying the room; there appeared to be nothing more to learn.

Boots pounded the corridor. Rader and Will Dawson charged in. The sheriff let out a scandalized roar.

"Ain't nothing sacred any more?" he bawled. "Burglin' the courthouse! Slade, do you ever miss anything?"

"I stumbled onto this one by accident, as it were," Slade smiled reply. "I got to thinking that Cale might be lonesome here or would wish to go out for a while, so I moseyed over here. If it hadn't been for that darned spittoon I kicked out in the corridor, I might have gotten the drop on the hellions. As it was, they very nearly dropped me. All I managed to do was drill a few holes in the wall."

"But you kept them from grabbing off the money," said Dawson. "Reckon that was considerable."

"I got the breaks," Slade replied.

"And made a few of your own," grunted the sheriff.

By the time the doctor arrived, Klingman was muttering with returning consciousness. A little later he was sitting up, holding his bandaged head in his hands and swearing.

"All I know is that I was sitting over by the window and all of a sudden the roof fell in on me; I don't rec'lect anything else," he answered the sheriff's question.

"Teach you not to sit with your back to

189

windows," snorted Rader. "What about him, Doc?"

"Let him go to bed and sleep off his headache," replied the doctor. "He's got a skull like a razorback; you couldn't dent it with a sledge hammer."

Slade gave the safe a careful once-over. "Four holes drilled," he announced. "A couple more and they would have lifted the knob."

"And lifted fifty-thousand dollars," added Rader. "I hope that bank messenger shows up early. The sooner that *dinero* is out of my hands the better I'll feel. Wallace, you and Jasper stay here tonight, and don't sit with your backs to the window."

"Do better than that, I'll close it," said Deputy Wallace, and suited the action to the word.

"And lock the door," added Jasper. "Crane, send over some coffee and sandwiches after a while, will you?"

"I'll bring 'em myself," promised the sheriff. "I want to keep an eye on you work dodgers, lest somebody steals the chairs from under you and leaves you sittin' on air."

"And be sure somebody doesn't wideloop the chuck off you on the way over," was the sarcastic rejoinder.

"Come on, Slade," said the sheriff. "We're in bad company here; that pair would contaminate a horned toad."

Slade left the office with Dawson and Rader. The door lock clicked behind them. Outside they found a gathering of the curious.

"Everything under control," the sheriff told them. "No, Klingman isn't bad hurt; he'll be okay in a day or so."

The Calaorra was rolling along as usual. They found a table, sat down and ordered coffee. Dawson drifted away to a poker game after a while. Slade and Rader sat smoking and watching the crowd. Norman Allen was not in evidence at the moment.

"The nerve of those sidewinders!" the sheriff suddenly burst out. "I never heard tell of the equal of it. Bustin' my safe with folks going and coming on a busy street and every now and then somebody going in or out of the building."

"I've a notion it may have been a good sign," Slade observed reflectively.

"What do you mean by that?" wondered the sheriff.

"I mean," Slade explained, "that, in my opinion, the head of the outfit is getting a mite desperate. He has to keep the money rolling in to hold his men in line, now especially after their nerve must be a bit shaken from the losses the bunch has suffered. That sort gets used to easy money mighty fast, and they get rid of it equally fast and are quickly hungry for more. If their leader can't keep it coming, they take to branching out

191

on their own, make blunders and everybody, including the boss, gets their come-uppance. He took a risky chance tonight in hope of recovering the bank loot they lost down in the gulley."

"Which means he's scared, eh?"

"I doubt if anything really scares him," Slade answered, "but I figure he is getting a trifle anxious; things haven't been going so well for him of late."

"If I was him I'd be making tracks to the Rio Grande and Mexico," said the sheriff. "Having—El Halcon on your trail's no joke."

"He might do just that, any time," Slade observed. "It's an eventuality I've been keeping in mind." He paused to roll and light a cigarette, then continued.

"The method employed to open the safe is interesting," he remarked thoughtfully. "That's foreign to the rangeland country, to all this Southwest section, in fact. A stick of dynamite, a little nitroglycerin or a sledge hammer with which to knock off the combination knob is the usual procedure. The drill is the tool of the expert cracksman who is familiar with the construction of safes and knows just how to operate the drill. An amateur could punch holes in the door all night and never get any results."

"Whoever it was must have known their business," said the sheriff.

"Yes," Slade agreed thoughtfully. "Means

also, unless I'm greatly mistaken, that they had experience in cities over east. Not often that sort drifts this far west, but as I said before, I'm confident the head of the bunch was either reared in or spent a good deal of time in eastern cities. I got only a glimpse at that pair and they were masked, but I'm willing to swear they weren't wearing rangeland clothes. Sure would have liked to get a look at their faces. Being masked indicates that they might well have been recognized by most anybody."

"A pity you didn't down the horned toads," growled the sheriff.

"Yes," Slade nodded. "I am pretty much of the opinion if I had, our problem would have been solved."

"You mean you figure one of them was the big skookum he-wolf of the pack?"

"That's my opinion," Slade answered. "Which indicates, I'd say, that he's really getting a bit frantic, taking a chance like that. Not that he lacks the nerve to take chances, any kind of chances, but such a thing just isn't good business. And he's a businessman and a good one."

"I hope you give him the business, and soon," growled Rader. "I'm hungry; I got jerked away from my breakfast before I had time to order any pie."

"Go ahead," Slade said. "I'll have some more coffee."

While the sheriff ate a leisurely meal, Slade went over, in his mind, his case against Norman Allen, overlooking no detail, evaluating pro and con every incident that served to tie up the saloonkeeper with the notorious syndicate. He was ready when the sheriff pushed back his empty plate and abruptly asked a question.

"Slade, do you really have a notion as to who is the head of the blasted outfit?"

"Yes," Slade replied, "more than a notion. I *know* who is the head."

"The devil you do!" exclaimed the sheriff. "Do you mind telling me?"

"No, I don't mind telling you," Slade answered. "I think the time has come for you to know. Now don't start, or look in that direction, but the man who is the head and the brains of your so-called syndicate just came out of the back room and is standing at the far end of the bar."

NINETEEN

Sheriff Rader's mouth dropped open slightly, his eyes widened. On his face was a look of incredulous disbelief.

"You—you don't mean Norman Allen!" he stuttered. Slade nodded.

"That's just who I mean," he said. "Norman Allen is the head of the syndicate, which is nothing but a regulation outlaw bunch with some novel ideas put into practice."

Rader shook his head. "Slade," he said heavily, "I'll usually go along with whatever you say and no questions asked, but this is just a mite more than I can swallow. What do you base your conclusions on?"

"I believe," Slade said slowly, "that I first got to thinking about him, although I hardly realized it at the time, when we came back from La Culebra that first night and you told him Yolanda was with Carter when he was killed. His habitual presence of mind forsook him and he looked rattled and apprehensive, almost scared."

"You mean he was afraid the girl would identify those hellions as associates of his?" interpolated the sheriff. Slade shook his head.

"No," he replied. "I don't think he paid her any mind. What if she did recognize them?

What could she do about it? Bring an accusation against Allen? The word of a dance floor girl against that of a reputable and well thought of businessman. Nobody would have paid any attention to her, and if they did, they'd surmise she was loco or had a grudge against Allen. No, he didn't bother about Yolanda."

"Then what did bother him?"

"Just this," Slade continued. "That razor-sharp mind of his immediately deduced that it was I who shot it out with Carter's killers. He was afraid I would be able to place them in company with him, and at the time he didn't know who or what the devil I was. When he learned that I was El Halcon, which he did very quickly, I imagine he felt greatly relieved, figuring that I was just another owlhoot trying to horn in on the good thing he'd started. That didn't bother him over much, at the time; he figured he wouldn't have any trouble taking care of me and proceeded to make a try at it. In fact that night I think he already knew the girl was with Carter; those standing off at a little distance to lend a hand if necessary must have told him. Then when he saw me dancing with Yolanda—just as she warned me I would be a suspect if seen with her—he or somebody got suspicious; I figured they would and perhaps tip their hand, that's why I danced with her. So he sent those two varmints to trail me and try and find out what I was up to. They didn't learn much."

"Just got the mortal blue blazes larruped out of them," chuckled the sheriff, "and got cashed in the following night."

"Yes," Slade nodded. "That pair undoubtedly had Indian blood and I've a notion it was they who knew about or discovered that old trail through the brush by way of which Dawson's cows were run off. As I said, I only vaguely thought about Allen at the moment; I was concentrating on Serge Kendricks. But Kendricks just didn't seem to fit into the picture in the right way. He's intelligent, but from the start I didn't credit him with the kind of brains needful to boss such an outfit. When the phony fight started in his place, his reaction was not that of a leader of men. He just barged in like a wild bull, swinging promiscuously without trying to get to the heart of the matter and take care of the ones who started the row. Quite a contrast to Allen's procedure during the row here earlier in the evening. *He* knew just what to do and how to do it; didn't make a single mistake and had things under control in a matter of seconds. And when that cowhand reached for his iron, Allen didn't go off half-cocked and drill him. His mind never ceased to function clearly and he just stood and waited until the other would make it plain that he, Allen, shot in self-defense."

"Just as when he killed Jack Richardson," the sheriff commented, his eyes sparkling with interest. "He waited for Richardson to reach before he pulled."

"Yes," Slade nodded. "That was something else to which I gave considerable thought. Not only did it show that Allen is extraordinarily fast and accurate but, in my opinion, according to your account of the affair, it also showed that he had once been associated with Richardson, an outlaw, and that there was bad blood between them. There was never any hint in Richardson's record of his being a robber. And it appeared that he went for Allen the moment he clapped his eyes on him. All conjecture on my part, of course, but important in the light of subsequent events; but I'm getting a bit ahead of myself in dealing with Allen."

He paused to roll and light a cigarette, then resumed:

"As I said, Allen had made up his mind to eliminate me as quickly as possible. Planting that stick of dynamite at the stable door was a little example of his methods. Nothing to tie up that with him, though. But do you remember the night Dawson invited me to visit his place and I promised I would the next day? Well, you and Allen were the only ones who heard me say that. It is pretty safe to assume that neither you nor Dawson made mention of it to anybody, but when I did ride for his place the next day, a nice trap was set for me to walk into, and I did walk into it. And remember the scar-faced varmint who tried to knife Serge Kendricks? Yolanda recalled him talking with men at the end of the bar, where Allen was standing. Another tie-up, although of course it could mean little. And three men who had been in Allen's company left the bar just after Serge and Yolanda departed, and I got a hunch to keep an eye on that pair who couldn't see anything but each other."

Rader shook his head. "What next?" he asked.

"By time time, I figured *Senor* Allen was getting a bit frantic and due to make a slip," Slade resumed. "He made a bad one the night after the Pleasanton bank was robbed, when he dispatched that hellion I saw him talking with to warn the robbers that we were an our way to the cabin in the gulch. The smart thing would have been to just send them orders to sift sand away from there, but he thought he saw a way to get rid of me and throw another good scare into folks at the same time. He's absolutely snake-blooded and without the slightest respect for human life. So he arranged things so we'd get blown from under our hats when we started across the moonlit clearing."

"And if it hadn't been for you they'd have done it," growled Rader. "Makes me cold along the backbone just to think about it. Go on."

"Then the attempt to rob your office tonight," Slade concluded. "Just after you told me, within

Allen's hearing, that the money was in your safe, Allen went into his back room, ostensibly to work on his books, and locked the door behind him. He slipped out the back door, got one of his bunch and made a try at the safe. He was taking a chance and he knew it, but he also knew that he couldn't trust any of his hellions to drill that safe. That required an expert cracksman, which he evidently is, among other unsavory things."

As Slade progressed, step by step, in his arraignment of Norman Allen, the sheriff's expression of incredulity had gradually changed to one of bewildered amazement. He shook his head, tugged his mustache.

"Well," he said, "I never would have believed it, but the way you put it, I have to. You sure make out a case against him."

"But not one that would stand up in court," Slade replied. "So far I haven't a thing on him that a good lawyer couldn't tear to shreds."

"But what the devil you going to do about him?" the sheriff asked helplessly.

"Wait, and watch," Slade answered. "I repeat, he's getting desperate—it's even showing a bit in his face and eyes—and he'll very likely make a fatal slip, sooner or later."

"Or you'll make it for him, I bet," Rader predicted confidently. "By the way, you're a deputy any time you want to be; I got the okay from the commissioners to swear you in."

"You may swear me in, but I don't want a badge and I *do* want you to keep it quiet for the present. I don't wish Allen to be on his guard any more than he is already."

"Okay," said the sheriff. "Hold up your right hand a mite from the table." He mumbled a few words. "There you are."

Slade nodded. "That'll give me all the authority I may need without revealing my Ranger connections," he said. "Now there's something else I want you to do. Dawson is a director and a big stockholder of the bank where Allen has his account. Have him keep a close watch, and if he learns that Allen has suddenly made a big withdrawal to get in touch with you at once. I've a feeling that with things going against him as they have of late, he may abruptly decide to pull out.

"And there's something I wish to caution you about," he added. "Be very careful not to change your attitude toward Allen, not in the least. If you do, that hairtrigger brain of his is very likely to catch on and cover up proper. Don't forget, now."

"I won't," the sheriff promised. "And you really figure he may take a notion to pull out?"

"I believe it's logical to think so," Slade said. "But I'm playing a hunch he may try to pull one more big job first. I hope so, that is if he doesn't get away with it."

201

"Surely can't be many of his bunch left alive," Rader commented.

"But, the chances are, the smartest," Slade answered. "We'll have our work cut out for us to anticipate and forestall whatever they may plan."

"You'll do it, no doubt in my mind as to that," Rader declared.

"Nice that you have such confidence in me," Slade smiled. "I hope it will be justified."

"It will," Rader said shortly.

Silence fell between them. Slade was trying to put himself in Allen's place, to figure what *he'd* do under similar circumstances. Long and varied contact with the outlaw mind enabled him to follow, to an extent, its devious workings. Allen undoubtedly had considerable money stashed away, but he was not likely to share it with his followers. But he must obtain money for them or he could no longer depend on their loyalty. As it was, their confidence in his ability as a leader and planner must have been somewhat shaken by recent events. A brilliant coup was needed to restore that confidence. If he pulled something big and got away with it, he could depend on his men for a while. Long enough to enable him to pull out, then very likely elude them and disappear from their ken. As the situation stood, he had nothing to fear from the law so long as one of his followers didn't make some disastrous slip or get his tail caught in a crack and start squawking.

All very well, so far as analyzing the situation went; but he still didn't have the slightest idea what Norman Allen might have in mind. He could only sit tight and await developments.

"What about Dawson?" the sheriff suddenly asked. "What am I to tell him when I ask him to keep an eye on Allen's bank account. It has to be justified, you know; bank directors aren't supposed to do such things."

Slade thought a moment. "I think we'd better take him fully into our confidence," he finally decided. "He can be trusted to be discreet, I'm pretty sure. But we must caution him, just as I cautioned you, not to change his attitude toward Allen."

"I think we can rely on him," said Rader. "He can keep a tight latigo on his jaw and he's not terrapin-brained. He'll string along with us without tangling the twine. I'll tell him to drop in at the office tomorrow afternoon."

Again silence fell between them and they sat smoking, each occupied with his own thoughts. Finally the sheriff left to walk around a bit and stretch his legs. Slade had several dances with Yolanda. In response to the pleading of Pedro, the orchestra leader, he sang a couple of songs for the gathering, which were received with the usual enthusiasm. After which he went back to his table to ponder the problem of anticipating and, if possible, forestalling Allen's next move.

What quirk of circumstance, he wondered, set such a man on the crooked trail? Norman Allen appeared to have everything needed to make a man a success in life. Undoubtedly he was a born businessman and in legitimate business could amass wealth and position. Why the overpowering lure of easy money, which in the end was seldom easy. Or was it a hatred of humanity in general, perhaps born from brooding over some past wrong, real or fancied. That could be the answer; Slade had known similar cases. The persecution of their family during and after the Civil War had started the James boys on their career of blood and violence. The murder of his brothers turned John Ringo into a bandit and killer, a hunted man who could not understand why his act of vengeance when he shot down his brothers' killers should put him beyond the pale of the law, which ever afterward he scorned and hated.

Or perhaps it went back farther. Perhaps when Norman Allen was put together, a faulty shard had been inserted in place of a clean-cut unit of character blending the creation to a perfect whole. Or— "Did the Hand then of the Potter shake?"

Slade sighed. Such speculation was wearisome and got him exactly nowhere. He left the saloon and walked slowly to where, beside the hallowed walls of the Alamo, he could see the clean beauty of the stars, symbols of Inscrutable Purpose.

TWENTY

Slade and Rader met with Dawson the following day. The rancher was less surprised at Slade's revelation than had been the sheriff.

"That jigger always seemed a mite too smooth to me," he said. "Always nice and doing the right thing, so far as anybody knew, always grinning; but somehow that grin never seemed to get to his eyes. I'm always a mite leary about a man who just skins his lips back to show his teeth, like a coyote. Don't seem just right to me. Now take that feller Kendricks at La Culebra. He's ugly as the devil wants to be, but when he grins, those green eyes light up and dance just like Slade's. Make you feel warm all over and give you the feeling that he's grinning with you, not at you. Allen is just the other way around. When he grins at me, I always feel he's making a darn fool of me, one way or another. And in a way I can't say anything against, which is worse than if I could rise up and belt him one."

Nor was he particularly surprised when told of Slade's Ranger connections.

"Should have knowed it from the beginning," he said. "You do things just like old Jim McNelty did when he was young. He was a ripsnorter in those days, was Jim. And don't worry, I'll keep everything under my hat. I only hope I get a chance to be in on the finish. Got a personal score to settle with the hellion. Two of my boys are still laid up from that ruckus in the cabin, you know, and I'm scared the one who got it through the shoulder will never be the same again; slug did a lot of damage to the muscles."

Several uneventful days passed. Slade walked about San Antonio, spent considerable time with Serge Kendricks and took a ride to Will Dawson's Triangle D *casa*. He rode watchful and alert, although he didn't really expect trouble; Allen hardly had enough men left to risk any of them on such an expedition.

Nevertheless, Dawson insisted on riding back to town with him, taking along several of his hands for good measure.

"Gives me an excuse to spend a night in town," he chuckled.

And then, the following day, Sheriff Rader came hurrying to Slade with news.

"He's going to pull out, all right," the sheriff stated excitedly. "Dawson just told me he's cleaned his bank account. Yep, you hit the nail on the head, he's going to pull out."

"Very likely," Slade agreed, "but the question is, what is he going to pull before he does pull out; that's what's got me bothered."

A couple more quiet days followed. Norman

Allen was his customary urbane self and showed no signs of nervousness or apprehension. The mocking smile was on his tight lips and he appeared to be enjoying some secret joke of his own. Which did not tend to enhance Slade's peace of mind.

Another day and Slade got a real surprise. He had dropped in for a chat with Serge Kendricks and found the saloonkeeper in a jovial mood.

"Well," he said, "I'm pulling out of La Culebra. Sold the place to my head bartender, on easy payments."

"The dickens you have!" Slade exclaimed. "Going into cow raising?"

"Eventually, but not yet," Kendricks replied. "Got me a new and better place; I'm taking over the Calaorra."

This time Slade really did stare. "Taking over the Calaorra!" he repeated.

"That's right," said Kendricks. "Norman Allen came over and offered it to me at what I considered a bargain price. Says he's leaving town soon, that he might open a place in Houston. The Calaorra is a nice place and gets a better crowd."

"And it will enable you to be closer to Yolanda," Slade observed with a smile as his mind raced to evaluate the surprising bit of information.

Kendricks chuckled. "Yolanda's leaving the floor," he announced. "She'll have her hands full looking after me."

"That I don't doubt," Slade agreed. "Everything in order concerning the transfer of the place to you?"

"Yes," Kendricks replied. "Judge Parkinson looked over all the papers and passed on them and looked up the title. Says everything is as it should be. I'm taking over tomorrow."

Sheriff Rader swore pungently when Slade relayed the news to him. "Yes, you were plumb right, he's going to pull out," he concluded, "and what are we going to do about it?"

"Nothing," Slade replied. "There's nothing we can do. He can ride out or take a train out tomorrow and we can only watch him go. There's not one iota of proof against him that would stand up in court. Try to stop him and we'd just make a laughingstock of ourselves."

"Then what *are* we going to do?" demanded the sheriff.

"I repeat what I said before," Slade answered. "Wait, and watch."

They waited, and they watched, to no avail. Norman Allen did leave San Antonio, three days later, by the Ten A.M. train, bound for Houston, or so he said. He dropped in at the sheriff's office, the mocking smile much in evidence, to bid Rader adieu.

"It's been nice to know a man of your—ah—capabilities," he said. "Goodbye, and good luck. And goodbye to you also, Mr. Slade. If you are

208

still capable of self-improvement, of which I am frankly unconvinced, if we should meet again, I expect you will be a wiser man."

Smiling and nodding, he left the office and headed for his train.

"The ornery sidewinder!" fumed the sheriff. "He knows he's got us where the hair's short and is making a joke of us."

Slade smiled. "I'm still playing my hunch," he said, "and I sure hope it is a straight one. I really believe it is," he added thoughtfully. "Let's go over to the Calaorra and eat. Haven't had breakfast yet."

The bank in which Norman Allen had his account, now one of San Antonio's largest and wealthiest, originated when a merchant accommodated his customers by hiding their money in a barrel beneath his floor. The bank had come a long way since those days and the money was now kept in a big but old-fashioned iron vault. The building which housed the bank was also old-fashioned and backed onto an alley. An elderly night watchman patrolled the structure, walking around it at regular intervals, but had never had anything to do other than make sure that doors and windows were locked and a fire kept going when the nights were cool.

He was strolling down the alley in back of the bank, some time well after midnight, when he thought he heard a sound in the direction of one of the windows. Holding up his lantern, he took a step in that direction and spotted a shadowy figure crouching against the wall.

"Hey, you," he began, dropping his hand to the butt of the old Smith & Wesson he carried. There was a whisper of sound behind him. A gun barrel crunched solidly on his skull and he fell, blood pouring from his split scalp. The man who wielded the gun bent over him.

"Nothing more to worry about," he announced. "Out like a light, and he'll stay that way. Let's go. Sam, you stay with the horses and if anybody comes nosing around, let him have it."

Three more men, all masked, materialized from the shadows. There was the scratching and scraping of a jimmy inserted beneath the window sash, a sharp click as the lock broke. The window was raised and the three men crawled through into the bank, where a dim light burned.

"One of you at each window," said the man who struck down the watchman, a tall and slender individual. He squatted before the outdated vault, produced a big brace and a number of bits of varying sizes, which he laid in order on the floor. Fitting one into the brace he applied the cutting edge to the vault door, placed the knob of the brace against his chest and began rotating the case-hardened bit, which cut into the soft iron as if it were cheese.

For more than half an hour he worked steadily, changing bits from time to time, while his companions watched at the windows and sounded no alarm. Finally he straightened up and lifted out the combination knob. A little more work with the drill and he seized the handle of the door and turned it. A moment later, the door swung open.

"Come on," he called in a low voice. "Bring the pokes and clean it."

The slide of a bull's-eye lantern was opened, the beam flashed about the vault. Packets of bills and sacks of coin were transferred from their resting places to stout canvas sacks which soon plumped out. The tall leader straightened up.

"Guess that's all that's worth taking, and it's plenty," he said. "Outside, now, and away we go."

The trio clambered through the window, sped to where a fourth robber waited with the saddled and bridled horses. The sacks were stuffed into saddle pouches, the quartette mounted, whisked off their masks, their faces a whitish blur in the gloom, pulled their hatbrims low and rode swiftly down the alley, headed west.

A light rain began to fall. The cold drops beat on the watchman's upturned face. He moaned softly, rolled his bloody head from side to side with returning consciousness. Dazedly he sat up and glared wildly about him. After a couple of fruitless efforts, he got to his feet and stood weaving. Gradually his numbed brain cleared somewhat. He stumbled to the window, peered in and saw the vault door standing open. Gathering himself together, he set out at a shambling run for where the sheriff slept.

TWENTY-ONE

Slade was awakened by the sheriff pounding on the door and calling his name. He opened it and Rader stormed in.

"They did it!" he bawled. "Busted open the bank and cleaned the vault. Must have got a hundred thousand dollars, maybe a lot more; can't tell till the cashier checks."

Slade began throwing on his clothes. "How many were there?" he asked.

"Watchman figured there were four or five of them, couldn't say for sure, got belted over the head and knocked cold. Rain brought him back to his senses," the sheriff answered.

"Go to the telegraph office and have them send wires to all the trail towns," Slade directed. "I don't think it will do any good, but we're not missing any bets. I think you will find Dawson at the Calaorra; I left him playing poker not long ago. If some of his hands are there, and I think they will be, get them for a posse. Otherwise, rouse up your deputies. Three or four should be enough with you and Dawson and myself. Be ready to ride as soon as you can. I'll be outside the Calaorra before you are. And grab off some sandwiches and stow them in your pouches; we're liable to need them before we're finished."

Rader headed for the door, then paused. "You figure you know which way they went?" he asked.

"I'm playing another hunch," Slade replied. "I think it's a straight one. Get going!"

The sheriff hurried out. Slade finished dressing, belted on his guns and rolled a cigarette. Then he headed for the stable and Shadow. He was lounging in his saddle at the saloon hitch rack before the posse were routed out and ready to ride. It consisted of Will Dawson, the sheriff and four of Dawson's hands. Slade led the way west out of the city and turned into the trail which led to Dawson's ranch house.

"We're heading for that old Indian trail which begins at Dawson's south pasture," he explained. "Dawson, you tell us where's the best place to turn off."

"You don't figure they might head for that gulley where the cabin we had the ruckus in is?" the rancher asked.

"I'm hoping that they'll figure me to think just that," Slade replied. "It's the obvious route for them to choose, and because it is the obvious is why I'm discarding it. I believe they'll take the old trail, travel west on it and then turn south to reach the Rio Grande. It'll be light by the time we reach where the trail begins and with this rain falling I'm pretty sure I can tell if they did take it. I'm playing a hunch, as I told Rader. So far my hunches have worked out pretty well."

"Got a notion this one will work out, too," growled Dawson. "I sure hope so. I'm itchin' for a go at those snakes. We'll make the turning-off place in about twenty minutes; from there we'll head south by a mite west."

"I've a notion they'll think they're in the clear and won't push their horses too hard, seeing as they have a long ride ahead of them," Slade remarked. "I think we've got a pretty good chance to catch them up."

They rode on at a good pace. After a while, Dawson said, "Here it is, the shortest cut to the pasture, and the going isn't bad." Turning almost due south, they quickened the horses' pace a little.

The sky was graying, and with the approach of day the rain stopped. The clouds shredded and rolled away and the sky was the tenderest blue. Birds began to sing in the thickets. A little breeze shook down myriad rain gems from the grass heads. The east began to glow and the sun thrust a golden rim above the horizon.

"Getting a break weatherwise, anyhow," Slade commented. "Better visibility than if the rain had kept up."

"Plenty of good shooting light," added the sheriff. "Just wait till I line sights with those hellions! I'm still burned up over what Allen said to me when he left to catch the train; I don't like being made fun of."

"You'll have the last laugh, see if you don't," Dawson said. "I can feel it in my bones."

It was full daylight when they reached the pasture and the wall of thorny growth which flanked it on the west. Slade dismounted, quartered the ground and carefully examined the encroaching brush.

"Hunch was a straight one," he announced. "Plain to see where the wet grass was beaten down by horses' irons and hasn't dried enough to rise up again."

"To your eyes, I reckon," grumbled the sheriff. "I can't see anything."

"And here are twigs that were broken since the rain began," Slade added. "Sap is still oozing out of them. I figure they are between two and three hours ahead of us, but if they aren't pushing their horses I believe we'll overtake them before noon. Let's go!"

With difficulty they pushed their way through the thorny growth and reached the deep depression that wound up the hill slope.

"Not too fast," Slade cautioned. "We don't want to have our horses winded when we come up with the devils; may need all they've got to give before the finish. If we can gain a mile in five we should he okay."

When they reached the spot where the trail forked, Slade again dismounted and went over the damp ground of the newer trail.

"They kept on west," he said as he forked Shadow. "Chances are this track runs all the way through the brush country, and that's a lot of miles, before it peters out or veers south to the Rio Grande. I think they'll follow it until it ends. Lonely country and they'll run less risk of being spotted and word sent on ahead."

In the wide hollow where the fight with the wideloopers occurred, they paused to let the horses drink their fill from the little stream and had a swig themselves. Remounting, they continued across the hollow and up the far slope, munching the sandwiches they had brought with them in their pouches. The sun was high in the sky now and both men and horses were sweating freely.

"The red-eye is sure pouring out of me," a cowboy moaned. "Wish I hadn't downed that last snort."

"You'll be lucky if something else doesn't pour out of you before the day is done," Sheriff Rader predicted with grim humor that was not particularly appreciated by its recipient.

"New ground from here on, the hollow's as far as we got last trip, so everybody keep their eyes open for side tracks and such," Slade advised. "Don't want them to turn off somewhere and give us the slip. And a little later it would be well to do less talking and more listening, and to pay attention to bends in the trail. I don't think there's much danger of them anticipating pursuit, but it's best to be on our guard. The hellion we're trailing has plenty of savvy."

The posse fell silent. Only the drumroll beat of the hoofs and the jingle of bit irons echoing back from the chaparral walls broke the great noonday stillness. Slade eyed every bend in the trail with suspicion and was tense for instant action. He knew that his followers' nerves were tightening up in anticipation of what was to come. Sheriff Rader constantly tugged his mustache. Dawson jerked his hat up and down. The cowboys fiddled with their reins, leaned forward now and then to stroke a horse's neck.

The growing tension was communicated to the animals. They snorted, rolled their eyes, pricked their ears. And there was something hypnotic in the steady pound of the hoofs on the hard surface of the old trail. Slade's eyes ached with strain, his pulses quickened, but he gazed straight to the front and his hands betrayed no hint of nervousness.

The sun stood directly overhead, its hot rays pouring down into the brush-walled depression. The air was close, for the tall growth shut out every breath of wind. And the gray track wound on and on, silent, deserted. Although he knew very well that he wasn't, Slade began to wonder in spite of his better judgment if he were following a cold trail with the outlaws hightailing along some other route. He cursed his vivid imagination that visioned them romping along, free from care, scores of miles from where he now was. He grew even more alert, however, as the track narrowed directly ahead and curved sharply around a dense bristle of thicket. He did not slacken spced, though, and they careened around the bend at a fast pace. Sheriff Rader let out an exultant bellow.

"Look! Look!" he shouted. "There they are!"

TWENTY-TWO

The trail had straightened out and ran for almost a mile without a bend. And far ahead were four dark blotches rising and falling against the gray background.

"Speed up," Slade called. "Maybe we can gain a little on them before they spot us."

The posse surged forward. Slade never took his eyes off the outlaws, who at the moment were not pushing their horses and apparently had no fear of pursuit. Nearly half a mile was covered and the forms ahead were taking on definite shape when he saw the white blur of a face turned to the rear.

That backward glance produced instant results. Slade saw the horses lengthen their stride, the riders bend forward, urging them to greater speed. The distance between the two groups became static. He settled his feet more firmly in the stirrups; the chase was on and it might well be a long one.

Far ahead was another bend in the trail. The outlaws whisked around it and out of sight.

"Get set," Slade called to his followers. "I don't think they'll stop, but take no chances and be ready for business."

They reached the bend, which proved to be

shallow and long, a steadily unrolling ribbon of threat. At any moment they might ride into the face of levelled rifles. However, that was a chance they had to take. Slow up and the quarry would gain precious distance. Slade believed therc was little likelihood of them stopping to shoot it out, but they might. He loosened his Winchester in the boot and his eyes never left the constantly approaching wall of brush ahead.

A general sigh of relief arose as the trail straightened out and again they saw the fugitives flogging their horses and glancing back over their shoulders.

"We've gained a little more on them," Slade said, "but there's still a long way to go."

"Getting pretty close to rifle range," observed Dawson.

"Still too far," Slade answered. "We'd have to slow up to do anything like accurate shooting| and that would allow them to pull ahead. No, ride and ride hard. Very likely everything will depend on whose cayuses give out first."

"That one of yours won't give out," grunted Dawson. "If you'd let him go he'd be right on top of them in another mile."

"Perhaps," Slade conceded, "but odds of four to one are a mite lopsided and I prefer not to buck them unless I have to. I believe we're a mite better mounted as a whole, except for that red sorrel the jigger in front, who I figure must be

Allen, is forking. He's holding back in deference to the others or I'm much mistaken."

Another bend, and another period of anxiety, but when at last they rounded it the distance between pursuers and pursued had lessened appreciably. Slade measured the stretch of trail with his eyes.

"A little more and we can risk throwing some lead at them," he decided. "Look out! They figure to do some throwing themselves."

One of the outlaws had twisted in his saddle. There was a puff of smoke and a slug sang past, high overhead. The posse instinctively ducked. They ducked again as a second bullet came closer.

"Can't we have a try at them now?" Dawson asked anxiously.

"Just a little more," Slade said.

"That devil on the sorrel is pulling ahead!" the sheriff exclaimed. "Yes, he's pulling ahead of the others, sure as blazes."

"Would be just like him," growled Dawson. "Ditch 'em to save his own hide. Wow! That one came close!"

Slade again measured the gap with his eyes. "All right," he said, "let them have it; long shooting but maybe we can cool them down a bit before they score a lucky hit." He slid his Winchester from the boot as he spoke. "Steady, Shadow," he told the black, who instantly levelled off in a smooth running walk. Slade clamped the rifle butt to his shoulder and let drive; the others followed suit. They saw the outlaws duck. Two more opened fire, but the rider of the big sorrel never turned his head; he was now several hundred yards ahead of his companions and steadily drawing farther and farther away from them. Slade eyed him anxiously between shots. His companions' rifles were banging away a fusillade, but without results; it was long shooting from the back of a moving horse.

For a mile the running battle continued, with the sorrel still gaining distance. A cowboy suddenly cursed shrilly, slewed sideways, let go his rifle and grabbed the saddlehorn to keep from falling.

"Got me through the arm!" he gasped.

"Stay with us," Slade told him. "Take care of you soon as we can." He levelled the Winchester as he spoke, his gray eyes glanced along the ights.

The rifle bucked against his shoulders and even as flame spurted, one of the outlaws spun from his saddle, hit the ground and lay motionless. His rifle flipped from his grasp.

"Watch him," Slade cautioned. "If he reaches for his six, let him have it again."

However the outlaw lay without motion as they swept past. Another moment and a second fell, almost in unison with a cowhand who slumped sideways and thudded to the hard surface of the trail. Dawson swore viciously and pulled trigger as fast as he could work the ejection lever.

The third rifleman suddenly jerked his mount to a sliding halt, whirled him and sat with both hands in the air.

"Hold it!" Slade shouted. "Take him prisoner, Rader. I'm after Allen."

His voice rang out again, "Trail, Shadow, trail!"

Instantly the great horse extended himself. His steely legs shot back like steam-driven pistons. He slugged his head above the bit, snorted, rolled his eyes and shot forward as if he had not already covered a great number of gruelling miles. Slade glanced at the mounted outlaw as he flashed past. The man sat motionless, hands above his head, as the posse surged up to disarm and bind him. Slade sheathed the Winchester and gave his whole attention to getting the last modicum of speed from his straining mount. Allen was nearly a half mile to the front and going like the wind. Slade settled himself to ride as he had never ridden before.

For in the tall red horse Shadow had for once very nearly met his match. Very nearly, but not quite. Slowly, almost imperceptibly, but steadily he closed the distance. The miles fled past and neither animal showed signs of exhaustion. Shadow's glossy coat was reeking with sweat, his eyes were gorged with blood, his nostrils flaring red, but with unabated speed he hurled himself forward, glaring at the horse that had the effrontery to think he could outdistance him. Slade encouraged him with voice and hand.

"You're doing it, feller," he exulted. "We've already cut that half-mile lead nearly in two. Just a little more and we'll try and smoke him out. We'll try and let him start it, though; that way we'll gain a mite more on him."

Shadow snorted as if to say, "Fine! only if you let him start it he may finish it before you get into action; better not take chances."

Slade chuckled, leaning forward in the saddle, estimating the distance which separated him from the quarry. Only a few hundred yards ahead of the flying sorrel was a bend in the trail. Slade hesitated, decided to let Allen reach the next straight-away before opening fire.

Allen careened around the bend, leaning far over in the saddle, and vanished from sight. Slade urged Shadow to one final effort.

Gallantly the black horse responded, giving his all in that last supreme test of courage and strength. With unabated speed he reached the beginning of the curve, his hoofs beating a wild melody from the hard-packed soil.

Slade leaned forward, his eyes fixed on the unravelling ribbon of the trail. Swerving around the last segment of the curve, he put forth every atom of his strength to haul Shadow to a slithering halt.

For there waiting for him was Norman Allen, sitting his blowing horse like a statue, right hand spread claw-like against his breast.

Fast as he was, Slade knew he could never hope to beat that lightning draw, and didn't try. He hurled himself sideways from the saddle as Allen's hand flashed to his armpit. Slade's hand gripped the stock of the Winchester as he fell. His life depended on the rifle not sticking in the boot.

It slid free. Prone on the ground, Slade threw the Winchester forward and fired as Allen's second bullet kicked dust into his face. He saw Allen reel, fired again. The two slugs crossed in Allen's body. Slowly he slid from the saddle and fell, his arms widespread. His gun dropped to the ground. The fingers of his right hand scrabbled in the dust in a vain attempt to reach it, then fell back as if utterly weary.

Slade got to his feet and walked to where Allen lay and knelt beside him. Allen glared up with glazing, hate-filled eyes.

"So you're taking over," he gurgled. "May you end up in the hell where I'm going!"

Slade slowly shook his head. He drew something from a cunningly concealed secret pocket in his broad leather belt and held it before the eyes of the dying man.

Allen's fading eyes dilated as he stared at the famous silver star set in a silver circle, the feared and honored badge of the Texas Rangers. His lips moved and a whisper of sound came forth,

"El Halcon—a—Ranger!"

"Yes," Slade said, "undercover man for McNelty's company."

Allen continued to stare at the symbol of law and justice. One last breath of sound seeped past his stiffening lips.

"You—can't—win. You can't win—against—the Rangers!"

His eyes closed wearily, his body relaxed, and he was dead.

For a long moment Slade gazed at the dead face. Not even death could erase the mocking smile from Norman Allen's lips. Straightening up, he walked to where Shadow stood with hanging head and heaving sides. Methodically with his hands and a brush from his saddle pouch, he gave the black a rubdown, then performed a similar ministration on the red horse, which was also exhausted. The chore completed, he leaned against Shadow's shoulder and rolled a cigarette. He was standing there, smoking when Dawson and Rader surged around the bend and halted their staggering horses.

"Did you get him?" the rancher called.

"Yes, I got him," Slade replied tonelessly. "I got him," he repeated. "A man who had every-thing, except—a conscience. I think you'll find a lot of the bank's money in his pouches, the way they're plumped out."

"The others are plumped out, too," said the sheriff. "I've a notion we recovered all of it."

"Where are the boys?" Slade asked.

"Left 'em back there with the prisoner, and skalleyhooted after you," Dawson answered. "Figured if the three of us couldn't handle the hellion nobody could. No, nobody hurt over bad. Gonzales, who got creased alongside the head and knocked out for a minute, was already on his feet, cussin'. The boys'll plug up the hole in Hartsook's arm. What about Allen?"

"Tie him on his horse, if you don't mind," Slade requested. "We'll take him with us."

Dawson and Rader performed the chore. After which they rode slowly back to the waiting cowboys. Slade examined the wounded, replaced the rag tied around Hartsook's arm with a clean bandage and smeared Gonzales' bullet-cut head with ointment.

"That should hold you till we get to town," he said.

Sheriff Rader approached the prisoner, who appeared willing to talk.

"Where'd you tie up with Allen?" he asked.

"In Colorado," the man replied. "We worked through Colorado and Oklahoma with him— he'd been everywhere and was smart. When things got a mite hot up there we drifted down this way. Allen set up in business and figured a new way to get money. We were doing all right for a while, until—" he shot a venomous glance at Slade.

" 'The wicked shall flourish like the green bay tree,' " quoted the sheriff. "But remember, the bay tree withers overnight."

He turned to Slade. "Now what?"

"Guess we'd better be heading back to town," the Ranger replied, glancing at the westering sun. "We've got an all-night ride ahead of us."

"Suppose you'll be pulling out now, eh?" remarked the sheriff as they got under way. Slade nodded.

"Yes," he said. "Captain Jim will have another little chore lined up for me, the chances are, by the time I get back to the Post. And I've had enough of this section for a spell; too wild and woolly for me."

"It's a lot less woolly than when you squatted here," the sheriff observed dryly. "I've a notion I can settle down to a peaceful life."

"I doubt it," Slade replied with a smile. "San Antonio never was noted for peace and quiet, and the chances are it never will be. Just the same, I rather enjoyed my visit and met some nice people."

"And some that were not so nice," grunted Rader, and dropped back to talk some more with the prisoner.

"You hit the nail on the head every time," he said when he rejoined Slade, a little later. "Allen was a safe cracker, the feller said. Born and brought up in Chicago, where I reckon he learned plenty of tricks. Feller said he and Jack Richardson met when they were both dealing cards on a Mississippi river boat. They had words and Allen put a hole through Richardson's gun hand. Richardson didn't forget and when he walked intotheCalaorra that night and saw Allen, he went for his gun. Allen beat him to the pull. Feller 'lowed there wasn't a man alive who could shave him on the draw. Could be, but I've a notion you could have at least broke even with him."

"I didn't care to try," Slade smiled. "Not much satisfaction in breaking even. That's like racing a railroad train to a tie at a crossing. Did the prisoner happen to mention why Bruff Carter was killed?"

"Uh-huh," nodded the sheriff. "Said Carter was getting suspicious of Allen's methods of doing things and Allen figured it was best to get rid of him in a way that would cause folks to hold the syndicate responsible. He was plumb snake-blooded."

Daylight was brightening the sky when they reached San Antonio. Utterly weary, Slade went to bed without delay and slept till mid-afternoon. After breakfast he visited the sheriff's office and found Rader already up and busy.

"The bank folks are anxious to have a talk with you and show their appreciation," he announced. "You saved them more than a hundred thousand pesos. And quite a few prominent gents would like a chance to congratulate you for bustin' up the blasted syndicate."

"You take care of them," Slade replied. "I'm riding as soon as I say goodbye to Kendricks and Yolanda. Tell Dawson and everybody 'so long' for me."

He repaired to the Calaorra, where Kendricks and Yolanda expressed their regret at seeing him go.

"Sure wish you'd stay with us," said the former. "We've been talking it over and I'm all set to offer you a piece of the place if you'll just consent to stay and help me run it."

"Thanks," Slade smiled, "but I've got itchy feet and have to be moving along ever so often. I'll be seeing you both sometime, I hope."

They watched him ride away, tall and graceful atop his great black horse, to where duty called and new adventure waited. Yolanda sighed.

"Honey, I've a notion you'd like to be riding with him," Kendricks said teasingly.

"Serge," she replied, "there goes what every girl dreams about and never expects to see. But you can't live on dreams and I like to eat. Come on, darling, I'm hungry."

Center Point Large Print
600 Brooks Road / PO Box 1
Thorndike, ME 04986-0001 USA

(207) 568-3717

US & Canada:
1 800 929-9108
www.centerpointlargeprint.com